Nancy Drew
on campus™ #22

In and
Out of Love

Carolyn Keene

AN ARCHWAY PAPERBACK
Published by POCKET BOOKS
New York London Toronto Sydney Tokyo Singapore

This book is a work of fiction. Names, characters, places and incidents are products of the author's imagination or are used fictitiously. Any resemblance to actual events or locales or persons, living or dead, is entirely coincidental.

AN ARCHWAY PAPERBACK *Original*

An Archway Paperback published by
POCKET BOOKS, a division of Simon & Schuster Inc.
1230 Avenue of the Americas, New York, NY 10020

Copyright © 1997 by Simon & Schuster Inc.
Produced by Mega-Books, Inc.

ISBN: 0-671-00214-7

First Archway Paperback printing July 1997

10 9 8 7 6 5 4 3 2

NANCY DREW, AN ARCHWAY PAPERBACK and colophon are registered trademarks of Simon & Schuster Inc.

NANCY DREW ON CAMPUS is a trademark of Simon & Schuster Inc.

Cover photos by Pat Hill Studio

Printed in the U.S.A.

IL 8+

In and
Out of Love

CHAPTER 1

"She actually sent us flowers?" Nancy Drew laughed in amazement as she clutched the collar of her terry-cloth robe in one hand.

Nancy was standing in the doorway of suitemate Casey Fontaine's room while Kara Verbeck, Nancy's roommate, was stretched out on the stripped bed across from Casey's. The morning sun streamed in through the windows of Casey's room, and the chatter of students heading out to their Thursday morning classes wafted up from outside to the third floor.

"Can you believe it?" Kara said, echoing Nancy's shock. Kara hid her pretty face in her hands and shook her head in disbelief.

"Just listen to this." Casey held up her hand for attention. Standing at her desk in black leggings and a T-shirt, she gestured at the huge arrangement of exquisite flowers that had been delivered five minutes earlier. There was a small envelope addressed, To the girls of Thayer suite 301, and signed, Stephanie Keats-Baur, Paradise.

Raking her fingers through her artfully disheveled red hair, Casey smiled as she read the card out loud.

" 'Dear Girls—Jonathan and I had a wonderful honeymoon. We took long walks, ate oysters, and spent hours sitting in front of the fireplace at the inn. Thanks for my bridal shower. What a surprise! I feel like the luckiest girl on earth! I'll be over soon to visit. Hugs and kisses, Stephanie.' "

Kara bolted upright. "Hugs and *kisses?*" she repeated. "What has happened to that girl? That's not the Stephanie who came here at the beginning of the semester."

"And she's coming back to visit?" Nancy asked with mock horror. "How soon?"

Casey laughed, then waved for them to stop. "Wait, there's a PS. 'By the way, married life is better than I ever imagined!' "

Nancy shook her head. The idea of man-crazy Stephanie Keats married—or even sticking to one man for more than a weekend—was amazing and kind of heartwarming. Kind of appalling, too, she thought.

Stephanie had met Jonathan Baur at Berrigan's department store, where she had taken a part-time job. Jonathan was her floor manager, and it had been love at first sight—at least until

Stephanie couldn't deal with the fact that she was dating just one guy. After continuing to hop from guy to guy for a while, she finally decided that it was time to grow up and make a commitment to someone.

Her decision hadn't been the height of romance, Nancy thought, or maturity.

Still, the entire suite, along with Casey's Kappa sorority sisters, had thrown Stephanie a shower and helped her to put together a wedding ceremony at the Kappa house.

"Stephanie in a white wedding dress . . ." Nancy mused out loud.

"I wouldn't have believed it if I hadn't seen it with my own eyes," Kara said.

"And everything happened so fast," Nancy said.

"So she wouldn't have time to change her mind." Kara giggled.

"But it *was* beautiful." Casey sighed. "They looked so much in love. Maybe their marriage will really last."

Nancy eyed Casey with interest. She knew that her suitemate had had her own struggles deciding when to tie the knot, ever since her movie-star boyfriend, Charley Stern, had proposed. Casey had decided she wasn't ready, and she and Charley were in a state of "permanent engagement."

Nancy couldn't even imagine *thinking* about

marriage at this point in her life. Especially since she wasn't dating anyone at the moment.

Suddenly Casey seemed to snap out of her daydream. "Well, we'd better get used to life without Stephanie, girls," she said firmly, glancing at Stephanie's old bed. "I got a memo from Campus Living saying that her replacement will be here as early as tonight."

"Really?" Nancy said, surprised. She took a comb out of her bathrobe pocket and pulled it through her long red-blond hair. "What's her name?"

Casey shrugged. "The note didn't say."

Kara swung her legs over the edge of the bare mattress and gave it a bounce. "Well, whoever sleeps here tonight couldn't possibly be as difficult as Stephanie."

"Or as entertaining," Nancy chimed in. "At least with Stephanie we knew what to expect."

"Yeah, the unexpected." Casey laughed, then glanced toward Nancy again. "Speaking of replacements . . ."

"Uh-oh," Nancy interrupted her friend. "I think I know what's coming."

Casey grinned. "I was just going to ask if you've gone out with anyone since Judd left."

Nancy's love life at Wilder had been like a roller-coaster ride. After breaking up with her high school boyfriend, Ned Nickerson, she had gone out with her rival at the campus newspaper, Jake Collins. After that didn't work out, she got interested in Judd Wright, who had just left Wilder for Cal State and a full track scholarship.

Nancy shook her head. "No. But it's okay," she told Kara. "I'm not really looking for a new boyfriend right now."

Kara stood up. "Judd's transferring so soon after you guys met was a real bummer," she said sympathetically.

Nancy shrugged, trying to make the best of it. "Cal State has one of the top track programs in the country," Nancy told her friends. "Judd will be happier there."

"But what about you?" Casey asked.

"If Judd's happy, I'm happy. Especially now that suite three-oh-one is going to have a new face to liven things up."

Just then she spotted Casey's clock on her desk. It was almost nine. She whirled around and headed out into the hall to go to her room. "I've got to get going," she called over her shoulder. "I have a meeting at the Student Union in five minutes!"

"Forty-eight, forty-nine . . . fifty!" Jake Collins, barefoot in blue jeans and a sleeveless T-shirt, collapsed facedown on his living-room floor. He rested for a second, then sat up, catching a glimpse of his reflection in the blank screen of the TV. His brown hair was tousled, and sweat beaded his forehead. Jake had been working out hard for over an hour.

"What a stud," a sardonic voice quipped behind him.

"Huh?" Jake said, startled. His roommate, Nick Dimartini, stood wrapped in a giant bath towel in the doorway, the right half of his hair crushed and his face creased from deep sleep. "Did I wake you?" Jake asked apologetically.

"No," Nick said groggily, rubbing his eyes. "I was wide-awake, doing calculus."

"Sorry," Jake said sheepishly. He *had* woken Nick. "I'll try to be quieter."

Nick collapsed on the couch. "What's wrong with you, Collins? It used to take a convoy of dump trucks to wake you. But the last couple of weeks you've been up early and bouncing off the walls."

Jake hopped to his feet and strode over to the refrigerator to pour himself a glass of juice. He downed it in four gulps. "Nothing's the matter," he said finally.

"Oh, really?" Nick replied doubtfully. "Then why are you so hyper all the time?"

"Purpose and energy are a bad thing?"

"They are in you!" Nick said. "Frankly, I'm worried."

"I'm not hyper," Jake shot back. "I'm working out a lot. I just want to get in good shape."

"Since when?" Nick demanded.

Jake searched the ceiling. "Since—I don't know. Since whenever."

"I'll tell you whenever," Nick replied. "Since you and the female race called it quits."

"I didn't call it quits with the whole female race—"

"Okay," Nick corrected himself. "Since Nancy dumped you."

Jake felt a bolt of unexpected emotion. "She didn't dump me!" he yelled.

A wry smile tugged at the corners of Nick's mouth. "Touched a nerve, did I?"

"Girls and I just aren't getting along at the moment," Jake said more calmly. "It's nothing serious. Just a little temporary misunderstanding. I don't understand them and they don't understand me. So I'm just taking a timeout." He glared at Nick. "But Nancy definitely did *not* dump me."

Nick held up his hands in mock surrender. "Whatever you say, Casanova. I'm not trying to give you a hard time. It just bothers me to see you like this."

Jake softened and sat on the couch next to Nick. "Maybe I am a little wound up," he admitted.

"Why don't you spend more time at the newspaper?" Nick suggested.

"No way." Jake shook his head. "Nancy's there all the time. Her stories are so good that Gail 'Editor-in-Chief' Gardeski throws her almost every big lead. I don't mind running into Nancy every once in a while, but seeing her every day is kind of depressing. She's so"— Jake struggled for the word—"so *happy*," he finished with a scowl.

"But Judd Wright is now oh-so-conveniently two thousand miles away," Nick pointed out.

"Judd Wright wasn't our problem," Jake muttered unhappily. He stood up and headed back to the kitchen, where he dumped some cereal into a bowl. "I didn't really get it, but I think Nancy just lost interest."

Nick shook his head at Jake's miserable expression. "Collins, you're in sad shape. You need someone new—and not someone five foot seven with gorgeous blue eyes and reddish blond hair."

Brown eyes would be nice, Jake said to himself. Shoveling a spoonful of cereal in his mouth, he nodded. Why fight it? he thought. I do need someone to distract me from Nancy.

So far, writing for the newspaper hadn't done the trick—neither had working out obsessively.

Jake carried his cereal bowl to the sink and rinsed it out. Finding a new woman was good advice. The problem was, Jake couldn't imagine anyone coming along who would be special enough to make him forget Nancy Drew.

"This is so nerve-wracking," Bess Marvin moaned as she paced the crowded hallway outside the drama department office in the Hewlitt Performing Arts Center.

"You'd better get used to it," her friend Brian Daglian warned. He put on a British accent. "This is the thespian life, after all."

"Sounds like a disease," Bess muttered, studying the small crowd that filled the hallway. Almost all the students in the drama department were there, and had been for as long as Bess. They were all waiting for Jeanne Glasseburg, a New York acting coach and visiting professor, to post the cast list for their next drama department production, *Cat on a Hot Tin Roof.*

"I don't think I can stand the suspense any longer," Bess said, searching in her pocket for a piece of gum or anything she could chew on besides her fingernails.

"Neither can the floor," Brian joked, giving her blond ponytail a playful tug. "Bess, you've been pacing this hallway for the past thirty minutes. And the audition wasn't for the part of the Energizer Bunny."

"Thanks a lot," Bess replied, narrowing her eyes at him. "Whenever I forget what it is I love about you, you always remind me with one of your supportive, nurturing, friendly comments."

"Which is not to say that if this *was* an Energizer Bunny audition, you wouldn't win hands down." Brian grinned. "Unfortunately," he added, "the production we're hoping to be a part of is *Cat on a Hot Tin Roof,* not *Bunny on a Hot Tin Roof."*

"And cats, of course, have been known to eat bunnies," a low voice drawled from behind them.

Bess turned and saw the star of the drama department, junior theater major Daphne Gillman. As usual, Daphne's hair was done in its glamorous 1940s style, making her look like Madonna impersonating Marilyn Monroe. And, as usual, she looked incredible.

"How nice of you to join the lowly masses," Brian teased. "I thought you didn't hang out waiting for cast lists to be posted."

"I usually don't," Daphne agreed coolly. "But that's just because I haven't had to worry about which part I got since my freshman year—when I started getting leads."

"Does that mean you're wondering about this lead?" Brian asked curiously. "Because I thought Bess's audition was pretty good."

Bess felt her face burning as Daphne turned to give her a long hard stare. Ms. Glasseburg herself had asked Bess to audition for Maggie, the lead, which had helped Bess feel positive about herself during tryouts. Bess thought her audition had gone well, but obviously, Daphne didn't agree.

After a moment Daphne relaxed. She smiled and shook her head at Bess like a mother scolding her child. "Yes," Daphne admitted.

"Bess had a nice audition. She should get one of the smaller roles."

Don't let her upset you, Bess told herself. Everyone knew that Daphne was confidence personified. And she was confident because she was talented. The problem was, she was also rude. Bess did her best to paste a smile on her face. "So, why did you show up to read the cast lists? What's the occasion, Daphne?"

"I just came because I thought it would be fun," Daphne said. "I'm not worried about my part, though. How could Jeanne pick anyone else to play a character as complex as Maggie? I mean, it must be obvious that there isn't anyone here who could play her as well as I could."

"Sure," Brian muttered. "So obvious that I didn't even consider it."

Bess didn't miss the sarcasm in Brian's voice. Still, it was hard for her to disagree with Daphne. After all, Daphne could definitely play the part of a sultry temptress like Maggie. She was tall, thin, and gorgeous. And then there was her acting ability. Most everyone agreed that Daphne was the runaway choice for the lead. She really would make a perfect Maggie.

"But I guess it's fun for you to see if you're going to be cast," Daphne continued.

"I guess I'll be lucky to get the role of the rug she walks on," Brian joked under his breath as he pulled Bess away. "Oh please,

please, let me be the rug or the floor. At least the doormat."

"I have the funniest feeling you wouldn't just lie there," Bess started.

Brian quieted her by squeezing her hand. Bess froze.

"The guessing game is over," he whispered. "Here comes Professor Glasseburg."

Nancy sprinted into the main sitting area at the Student Union, her book for her ten o'clock class in Western civ clutched to her chest. She'd spent so much time talking with Casey and Kara that morning that she'd almost forgotten about meeting a photographer from the *Wilder Times*. She'd had just enough time to throw on a pair of old jeans, a bulky Wilder U. sweatshirt, and a corduroy jacket that had once belonged to her father and get to the Union to meet Gary Friedman.

Nancy quickly scanned the clusters of tables, chairs, and couches, where students sat around studying or talking while they ate bagels and drank coffee.

Finally she spotted Gary kicked back in one of the easy chairs, a cup of coffee and a Danish beside him. He wore a baseball cap over his short hair with the bill low over his wire-rimmed glasses. He appeared to be asleep. At his feet was a black case filled with photography equipment. Nancy met Gary shortly after she had started working on the paper. He was a very talented photographer and had won prizes in national photography contests. Everyone at the *Times* loved working with him and being around his dry, ironic sense of humor.

"Sorry I'm a few minutes late, Gary." Nancy panted as she hurried toward him.

"Hey, Nance!" He pushed back his cap and motioned to the chair next to his. "Don't worry, my next class isn't for a half hour," he said.

As she sat down, Nancy noticed that Gary was a little pale, and that dark half-moons cupped the bottoms of his eyes. "Are you feeling okay?" she asked him with concern. "You look like you haven't slept for a week."

Gary squinted up at the ceiling. "Let me see. Has it been one week—or two?"

"Insomnia?"

Gary shook his head. "I have this psycho premed roommate, Trevor McClain, who likes to study around the clock. He's so intense. If he doesn't get a four-point-oh, he freaks."

Nancy nodded. "I know the type."

"Unfortunately, he hates libraries," Gary went on. "So, when he's not at the lab, he's in our room, studying. And while he studies, he listens to his Walkman, with the earphones over this stupid Toledo Mudhens baseball cap he always wears, and—"

"Wait!" Nancy jumped in before Gary could

13

finish. "Let me guess," she said. "He hums along with his Walkman!"

"Exactly," Gary said. "And let's just say Trevor's not exactly a gifted singer." He sighed. "Anyway, enough about me. What's so important that we had to meet this morning?"

As Nancy eyed Gary's Danish, she felt a plaintive rumble in her stomach. She hadn't had time to grab breakfast. "I just wanted to tell you your plans for tomorrow afternoon."

"My plans?" Gary asked. "How would you know my plans?"

"Because I just made them." Nancy smiled. "But everything's been okayed by Gail at the newspaper, and your *Wilder Times* calendar has been cleared. As of tomorrow afternoon you belong to me."

"I'm a little busy right now," Gary started to explain. "I'm doing this huge photo essay on campus housing—"

"I've heard about it," Nancy cut in. "It sounds like fun, but this job is even *more* fun," Nancy insisted.

Gary rolled his eyes. "Okay. What is it?" he asked.

Nancy poked his knee. "You'll love it," she told him again. "My friend George Fayne has a friend, Mara Lindon, who is putting together a really interesting exhibit on the history of women's athletics at Wilder University."

Suddenly Gary's eyes sparkled with interest. "Did you say Mara Lindon?"

"Oh, yeah, Mara Lindon. And I'm writing a feature on the show for the *Times,*" Nancy said breezily. "And you—"

"And I'm taking the pictures!" Gary finished.

Nancy nodded.

Gary gave her a suspicious look. "Did I, uh, ever happen to mention that I've had a little crush on Mara Lindon since the minute I laid eyes on her during this year's freshman orientation?"

Nancy grinned. "Oh, only about ten or twenty times," she said.

Gary gave her an embarrassed smirk.

She smiled back at him.

"So you're free tomorrow afternoon after she has tennis practice?"

"As you said, my calendar is completely clear," he replied.

"Good." Nancy stood up and waved good-bye to Gary, a satisfied grin on her face.

You're brilliant, Nancy Drew, she congratulated herself. Not only had she managed to get the best photographer on the paper to work with her on a story about women's athletics, she had also found a way to hook Gary up with Mara.

So what if your own love life has come to a major halt? Nancy thought. Maybe Gary's is about to take off!

CHAPTER 2

George Fayne's hair was still dripping from her postrun shower, when the phone rang.

Her roommate, Pam Miller, picked it up. "It's your mom," Pam said a moment later, holding the phone out to George.

George rolled her eyes as she rubbed a towel over her head. Then she took the receiver from Pam and sat down. "Hi, Mom."

George's mother had been calling almost daily, ever since George had complained to her about mysterious flulike symptoms she'd had. It was sweet the way her mother was worried about her. George could only imagine how much more worried her mother would be if she knew the truth—that for a few days, George had thought she was pregnant.

"Yes, I'm way over the flu now," George assured her mother.

George hated to lie, but her experience had

16

been hard enough without bringing her mother
into it.

"Good, honey," her mother replied. "Are
you getting enough rest?"

"Yes, Mom," George replied in a monotone.
"I know, I know. You can't study on an empty
stomach or with a tired mind."

George lifted her legs and crossed her bare
feet up on her desk, only half listening to her
mother. She was staring at a picture of Will
she had taped to the side of her computer
monitor. He was the epitome of gorgeous, with
jet black hair, bottomless black eyes, and a
burnished complexion.

Will was an amazing guy, and George was
glad that the two of them had worked out all
the complicated issues that had come between
them recently.

Even though George hadn't been pregnant,
she had decided that she wasn't ready to sleep
with Will again. He'd had some trouble dealing
with her feelings, but now he was being really
supportive. It was weird: now that she had
made the decision that she was too young to
sleep with Will, she felt more mature and
grown-up than before.

George blinked. Her mother had just asked
a question, and she wasn't sure what it had
been. She took a guess. "Uh—is Nancy coming
home to River Heights next weekend?" Bingo!

"I have no idea, Mom. Should she? You ran into whom? Avery Fallon?"

Oh, boy, Nancy's going to love *that*, George thought.

Avery was Nancy's father's new girlfriend, and Nancy hadn't exactly accepted her with open arms. In fact, George always suspected that it was the tension in the Drew household that had been at least partially responsible for Nancy's breakup with Jake Collins. Nancy had been the most important woman in Carson Drew's life for a long time, and sharing Carson wasn't easy for her. And apparently, after Nancy had brought Jake home with her, Jake hadn't been as understanding of Nancy's feelings about Avery as Nancy had expected.

But Carson Drew's birthday was coming up, and George's mother thought Nancy might be coming home for the occasion.

"I don't know, Mom," George said doubtfully. "But, yes, if she does go home, I'll ask her if she can bring back the warm clothes that you packed for me." George laughed as she realized why her mom was so interested in whether Nancy was going home for Carson's birthday. "Mom! You want Nancy to bring me a care package!"

Her mother didn't deny it.

"Have no fear, Mom," George continued. "I'll ask Nancy about her plans for her dad's birthday. Would you stick some of your trail-mix cookies in with the clothes?"

"Okay, people," Professor Glasseburg said as she approached the anxious group of students waiting to read the cast list. "If I can't get to the bulletin board, none of you will have a part in anything!"

As if by magic, a path opened for Professor Glasseburg to walk through to the bulletin board. Bess tried to edge her way to the front, but the path closed up quickly. It seemed that Professor Glasseburg had been swallowed up from behind by the throng of students. From where she stood, Bess could only see two hands floating above the crowd of heads as Professor Glasseburg tacked up the cast list.

Immediately, there was excited chatter all around Bess.

"I can't believe I've been waiting here all afternoon and now I can't even see," Bess complained, turning to Brian. But Brian was gone. Bess scanned the crowd and saw that somehow he had managed to get a spot up front.

"Yes!" he cried, pumping his arm into the air.

"Brian!" Bess shouted. "What is it? Did you get a part? Did I get a part?"

Brian pushed his way back through the

crowd, and when he reached her, he swept her off the ground in a whirl of excitement.

"Brian!" Bess cried, laughing at his antics. "Don't make me crazy. What happened? Did you get a part?"

"Did *I* get a part?" Brian said. "Only the lead male role, Brick!"

"Oh, Brian!" Bess gave her friend a huge hug. "That's great! But I never doubted you."

"So?" Brian said as he set her back on the floor.

"So what?" Bess asked.

"Aren't you going to ask me about *you?*" Brian went on in an exasperated tone.

Bess just stared at him. She was too afraid to ask him if her name had been posted.

Finally Brian grabbed her arm and pulled her into the crowd. Then he put his arms around her waist and hoisted her into the air.

"Can you see the cast list?" he shouted up to her.

Bess squinted. She could see the sheet of white paper attached to the bulletin board, but she was too far away to read what it said.

"Can you get me closer?" Bess yelled down to him.

Bess swayed over the heads of the people in front of her as Brian stepped closer to the board. Her eyes quickly scanned the list of names and she felt her heart skip a beat.

"Oh my gosh," she murmured, closing her

eyes for a second. "I must be dreaming or something." But when she opened her eyes again, the words were still there. Maggie— Bess Marvin.

"You're Maggie!" Brian exclaimed, setting Bess down and shaking her by the shoulders. "It's you and me, Bess, the dynamic duo!"

Bess just stared at him as he pulled her to a quiet corner. How had she done it? How had she gotten the part? And not just any part— the *lead!*

"Maggie, honey," Brian was joking. "Speak to me! Don't lose your voice now, Maggie, you have way too many lines to learn!"

"What do you mean, *'Maggie'?"* a voice asked suddenly.

Bess whirled around to see Daphne stalking toward them with a suspicious expression on her face.

"Are you saying that Bess got the lead?" Daphne demanded.

"That's right!" Brian crowed with pleasure. "You're looking at Maggie the Cat."

Bess stared at Daphne blankly. Bess had wanted a part so badly, but she'd never really believed she could land the lead. Finally, as if a dam had broken inside her, Bess found herself screaming and crying at the same time. She and Brian grabbed on to each other and jumped up and down. Bess was so excited, she completely forgot about Daphne, until Daphne spoke again.

"Obviously it's a pity thing," Daphne snapped. "I mean, her boyfriend dies and so not only does she get into Glasseburg's class— but she gets the lead in her play, too."

Bess froze. Everyone standing nearby could hear what Daphne was saying.

"Ignore her, Bess," Brian said quickly. "Daphne's jealous, that's all. Now, let's get out of here and go brag to all our friends."

Brian's right, Bess told herself. Don't let your insecurities and Daphne's nasty comments ruin one of the happiest days of your life.

She turned back to Brian and hooked her arm through his. "I'm very good at bragging," she said firmly.

"I always knew you had it in you," Brian replied.

Jake made his way through the lunchtime crowd that packed the quad. His roommate's advice about starting to date again was still ringing in his ears. And as he looked around, he had to admit that there were a lot of beautiful women on campus.

But no one like Nancy, he thought. He'd dated plenty of women before meeting her, but he'd never fallen so hard.

Jake stopped outside the *Wilder Times* offices and stared up at the second-floor windows.

I wonder if she's up there, he thought. Not that her presence should keep him away. After all, he was the paper's senior staff writer. He had just as much right—more even—than she did to be up in the *Times* office.

But who was he fooling? He knew that he hadn't felt totally comfortable at the paper since he and Nancy broke up. And seeing her with that Judd Wright had been really hard. The thought of Nancy with another guy, the thought of her arms around another guy's waist, her lips kissing his . . .

Stop it! Jake commanded himself. Just focus on yourself.

With that, he barged up the stairs to the office. Inside, he poured himself a cup of coffee from the machine and then headed for his cubicle.

The office was buzzing, as it did every Thursday, when the staff rushed around, trying to finish their stories by deadline. The *Wilder Times* came out every Monday, and everything had to be ready for printing by the end of Thursday.

"Jake!"

Gail Gardeski bolted out of her office with a pile of copy clutched in her hands. Usually dressed in conservative skirts or dresses, Gail was dressed down today, in jeans and a T-shirt.

"These pieces you turned in are good," she told him.

"Good," he said resolutely, "because I want more work."

Gail eyed him suspiciously. "You already write more than anyone else on the paper."

Jake threw a glance toward Nancy's cubicle, across the office from his. Her overhead light was on. He could see wisps of her red-blond hair over the low partition wall.

"Let's just say I have more time on my hands these days," Jake explained.

Gail sighed and put a hand on one hip. "Jake, I don't want to get in the middle of whatever's going on between you and Nancy," she said in a low voice, "but I don't want your personal life getting in the way of what you do here. You and Nancy are my two best writers, and—"

"Which is why I want *more* work, not less," Jake cut in. "I want to stay busy, Gail."

Gail thought for a minute, then bolted back into her office. When she emerged she was carrying a single sheet of paper, which she handed to him. "I was planning to assign this story to a freshman, but if you want it, it's yours."

"What is it?"

"An interview with a transfer student from Russia. She just arrived today, and the meeting's set for tomorrow morning at nine in Java

24

Joe's." Gail checked her notes. "She'll be wearing a red scarf."

"Wearing a red scarf?" Jake laughed. "What is she, a spy?"

Gail grinned. "She *is* from Russia. And I hear she's pretty interesting. By the way, I saw her picture." Gail's eyes glittered with mischief. "Actually, this may be just the kind of assignment you were looking for."

"I doubt it," he said glumly. "But at least it will keep me busy."

Jake looked down at the assignment sheet. "Nadia Karloff," he muttered. A moment later he felt his eyes roaming toward Nancy's cubicle, where he could hear her voice as she spoke to someone. She started laughing, as if she didn't have a care in the world.

Jake winced. It was a reflex. The sound of Nancy's laughter was as piercing as a train whistle.

Jake sighed as he leaned back and put his cowboy boots up on his desk. She's happy, he realized. She doesn't miss me one bit.

But here he was—wallowing in self-pity and begging for freshman assignments. You're pathetic, Jake Collins, he told himself. Totally pathetic.

CHAPTER 3

Bring us your best bottle of extremely over-priced water, please," George said with a flourish. "We're celebrating."

The waiter raised an eyebrow and sighed. Then he dutifully wrote down George's order and stalked away. A minute later he returned, showed the bottle to George as if it were a bottle of the finest wine, and poured her a taste. George ceremoniously took a sip and nodded her approval.

"Maybe I should go crazy and make it two bottles," George joked as the waiter filled the glasses. Nancy and Bess started laughing.

The three of them were at Les Peches, one of the most elegant restaurants in Weston. George and Nancy were taking Bess out to dinner to celebrate her getting the lead in the new play.

"Bess Marvin, you got the starring role," Nancy said. "And you're only a freshman."

"I know." Bess shrugged, grinning from ear to ear. "I still can't believe it."

"I'm so proud of you, Bess," George said. She reached out and gave her cousin's hand a squeeze. "You're really putting your life back together."

"And not just getting by, either," Nancy agreed. "You're kicking some you know what!"

"Some Daphne Gillman butt, you mean." Bess chuckled.

George couldn't be happier for her cousin. In the last few days Bess seemed to have finally shaken the lingering depression she'd had since her boyfriend Paul's death. Not that someone could ever be expected to recover completely. But it was nice to see Bess excited about something again.

"Here's a toast to Tennessee Williams for writing the play," George announced. All three lifted their glasses of high-priced water into the air.

"Now let's toast the lead," Nancy said. "To Bess Marvin, to Maggie!"

The trio clinked glasses again.

"I wouldn't want to share this moment with anyone else," Bess said happily. "You guys are my two best friends. Thank you."

Just then the waiter returned with a basket

of warm crusty bread and a saucer of olive oil and spices.

"And thank *you*, Bess," George added, reaching for a slice of bread. "If you hadn't landed the lead, we wouldn't have had an excuse to take you out for a fantastic dinner."

"Good celebrations don't come around that often," Nancy agreed.

"Speaking of celebrations," George said. "Are you going home for your dad's birthday?"

"That's right," Bess chimed in. "Your dad's birthday is coming up."

"Uh . . ." Nancy's face flushed, and she looked startled for a second. "I hate to admit this, guys," she murmured, "but I completely forgot about Dad's birthday."

George was surprised. "That's not like you, Nance," she said. "Your dad's birthday is usually one of the biggest events of the year for you."

"I know, I know," Nancy agreed, still flustered. "But ever since that long weekend when we all went home, things have been really strained between me and my dad."

"Because of Avery?" George asked gently.

Nancy nodded. "I know I shouldn't be angry about it," she admitted, pulling apart her slice of bread without eating it. "I mean he has a right to have a girlfriend and his own life."

Bess nodded. "He probably should have done this a long time ago," she said tentatively.

"I just can't get used to it," Nancy went on. "It's just so hard to know there's a woman in my father's life."

"You mean besides you and Hannah," George said with a grin. She was talking about Hannah Gruen, who had been the Drews' housekeeper since Nancy's mother died when Nancy was three.

Nancy smiled. "Right."

"Maybe his birthday is the perfect time for you to clear the air," George suggested.

Bess nodded. "Definitely. Or at least to do something to let him know that you love him."

Nancy stared at her friends thoughtfully. "You're both right," she said.

George's eyes twinkled. "But do you really think you can top the disco party we gave your dad when we were fifteen?"

"Or the birthday cake we helped you make when we were in fourth grade?" Bess reminded them.

"The one where we used regular soda instead of baking soda?" Nancy remembered, starting to laugh hysterically.

"That was one flat and soggy birthday cake!" George chimed in.

"Ugh, don't remind me," Nancy said as the waiter came to the table to take their orders. "I don't want to spoil my appetite."

"Let's plan something incredible," Bess said enthusiastically.

"That's right," George added. "At least now the three of us know how to make a birthday cake," she added.

"Right." Nancy laughed. "Buy it!"

"Here's Nancy!" Casey called out. "Now we're all here."

Nancy closed the door to her suite and looked around in surprise. All of her suitemates were gathered in the lounge. Casey and the hall's resident advisor, Dawn Steiger, were sitting on the couch. Kara, Eileen O'Connor, Reva Ross, and Ginny Yuen were lying on the floor. Liz Bader had dragged out her desk chair and was straddling it backward.

Sandwiched between Casey and Dawn was someone Nancy had never seen before. The woman was about Nancy's age and had raven black hair, doelike brown eyes, and high, Slavic cheekbones. Without a doubt, Nancy thought, this stranger was probably the most mysteriously beautiful woman she had ever seen.

"Hello," Nancy said tentatively.

Casey tilted her hands toward the new girl as if Casey were a game-show hostess displaying something. "This is our new suitemate, and my new roommate, Nadia Karloff."

"And she's so fascinating," Kara whispered.

Smiling, Nancy offered her her hand. Nadia's grip was firm and confident.

"A pleasure, Nancy," Nadia said, in a thick Russian accent.

As Nancy lowered herself to the floor, she felt Nadia's eyes on her. She seemed to be sizing Nancy up, trying to fit her into the puzzle of her new suitemates.

"Nadia was just telling us about herself," Casey explained. "You have to listen to this story, Nance. It's amazing."

Nadia's cheeks flushed with embarrassment, and her eyes were cast downward modestly. "No, no," she protested, motioning with her hands. "My family is like most in Russia."

"Her father got sent to Siberia," Casey interrupted. "He was a famous poet who wrote about the hardships of living under Communism. He spent ten years in a work camp for political prisoners."

"But then after perestroika, when things loosened up and the country started to embrace democracy," Kara continued, "he was released and started a liberal newspaper with Nadia's mother. He was the publisher and she was the editor, and Nadia and her older brothers and sisters worked as writers."

"Really, my family members are not heroes," Nadia protested in her charming lilt. "We just do what you have to do to survive. If my father did not write, he would be—how do you say it—like a fish out of water, and would die. And without my mother's strength, we are nothing. She wrote him every day in prison. And kept the six of us children fed and clothed. She made sure we did our studies."

"Doesn't it sound romantic?" Even Liz, a New Yorker who tended to be jaded about most things, sounded entranced by Nadia's story.

Nancy nodded, impressed. "Not romantic, really. But interesting—and hard."

"Hard, exactly," Nadia agreed, catching Nancy's eyes and holding them with an inquiring gaze of her own. "Nancy is right. Not romantic."

"Nancy's a writer, too!" Kara stated, giving her roommate's arm a proud squeeze. "She's the star reporter for the *Wilder Times.*"

Nadia sat forward. "Really?"

"Not the *star,*" Nancy said shyly.

"Don't be modest, Nance," Casey called out. The suitemates started telling Nadia about some of Nancy's articles. Suddenly Nancy caught Nadia's eyes. To her surprise, she felt an immediate bond. For some reason, she sensed that they had a lot in common.

"Nadia was just about to tell us why she's here at Wilder," Eileen said, changing the subject.

Everyone leaned forward eagerly.

"Well," Nadia began humbly, "my father and mother thought that I will one day take over their newspaper. They want me to come and get the best education possible, to learn

English perfectly, to get world—how do you say it?"

"Experience?" Nancy suggested. "World experience?"

Nadia nodded eagerly. "Yes. I am late to school because my parents insisted I travel around America before I stop in one place. I've been traveling for five months."

"You've probably seen more of America than most of us," Nancy commented.

"Do you miss home?" Casey asked.

Nadia began to nod her head very slowly. "Very much," she said, and patted her heart. "There is something called the Russian soul. It is not always comfortable in Russia, or warm, and we do not always have enough to eat, but the Russian people are very deep people. And I miss them."

The room fell silent for a moment as everyone nodded with respect and understanding.

Nancy detected other emotions in her new suitemate. While Nadia's words were sad, her beautiful face was expressing excitement.

A small smile tugged at the corners of Nancy's mouth. Maybe on the inside Nadia had an old Russian soul, but on the outside she looked American in her tight blue jeans, cowboy boots, and Norsemen sweatshirt.

"Well, Nadia," Nancy proclaimed, "welcome to Wilder U. And welcome to suite three-oh-one."

CHAPTER 4

On Friday morning Jake reluctantly got out of bed and crossed the living room to go into the kitchen. Nick stood in front of the sink, spooning coffee into a filter.

"I'll have a triple espresso and a cinnamon bun," Jake joked.

"You're up early," Nick remarked, ignoring his request. "I thought Friday was the day you allowed yourself to sleep in."

Jake yawned. "I have to do an interview."

Nick's eyes focused due north of Jake's eyebrows. "Then you'd better do something about that bed-head."

Jake smoothed down his unruly hair. "What's the point? I don't have anyone to impress."

Nick cocked his head. "Do I detect self-pity in your voice, or is that just false modesty?"

Jake reached for a coffee mug. "Self-pity,"

34

he said offhandedly. "I saw Nancy at the *Times* office yesterday."

"And—"

"And nothing. She never even checked to see if I was there. . . . But I don't care. I'm over her."

Nick eyed him incredulously. "Uh-huh. Yeah, I really believe you."

A short while later Jake trudged across campus sipping at the coffee mug he held in his hand. In the distance, he could hear the Wilder marching band practicing for Saturday's big football game against—against . . .

Whoa, Collins, he thought suddenly. You *are* out of it. He couldn't even remember who the Norsemen were playing, which was really strange because Jake had always been a big football fan. But like everything else these days, football just didn't interest him.

A second later Jake stopped and patted his pockets. "Oh, man!" he groaned. He'd forgotten his notebook and pen. And he'd left his tape recorder at the *Times* office. Now how was he going to do the interview?

"This Nadia person probably has nothing interesting to say, anyway," he muttered, walking on. "I'll just jot some notes on a napkin."

He smiled as he remembered what Gail said, that Nadia would be wearing a red scarf. That should make her easy to spot.

He stood outside the big window at Java

Joe's, his nose pressed against the glass. Most of the tables inside were full—with couples, he noticed.

He was about to head inside when he caught sight of a flash of color in the back of the little coffee shop. A flash of red. As Jake squinted through the window, his body seemed to register the sight before his brain did.

The red scarf was attached to a supple, sexy neck, which was attached to one of the most captivating heads he'd ever seen bent over a book. As the girl wearing the scarf sat up, he noticed her long, lithe body in tight jeans and black leotard top.

"Please be Nadia," he pleaded out loud. "Please be Nadia."

Eyeing his reflection in the glass, Jake wet his fingers and worked at his hair. Then he tucked in his shirt and straightened his jacket. He regretted not having shaved.

You're a reporter, he reminded himself. Reporters are supposed to look unshaven and mysterious.

As he walked into Java Joe's and made his way toward the red scarf in the back, Jake tried sending a telepathic message to his boss. Thank you, Gail!

"Don't keep your tummy pulled in, honey," Amanda mumbled around the pins in her mouth. Amanda was a theater major whose first love was costumes. She angled for the job of wardrobe mistress on almost every Wilder production. "The costume is a slip," she reminded Bess. "If I make it too tight, and you take any kind of deep breath later, you'll split the whole thing open onstage."

"Sorry," Bess mumbled. Embarrassed, Bess let out the air she'd been holding in, and Amanda let out her tape measure another inch. It was Friday morning, and Bess was back in the Hewlitt Performing Arts Center, at a costume fitting. Professor Glasseburg had said that she wanted all the actors to get into costume as soon as possible, to help them get into their roles and to help Bess get comfortable wearing just a slip onstage.

Amanda busily stuck pins in the slip and then held it up for Bess to see. "Personally, I'd never be able to wear something like this in public," said Amanda with a chuckle.

"Anything for art," Bess joked sarcastically under her breath.

Amanda took the pins out and basted the slip before handing it to Bess. "Why don't you try it on now so you can look at yourself as Maggie."

Bess pulled on the slip that would be all there was between her body and an audience of hundreds. The cool silk slid over her skin and made her shiver.

"Just as I thought—I'll have to do a little

more adjusting," Amanda said, reaching for her pins and kneeling on the floor in front of Bess.

Bess looked at herself in the mirror as the wardrobe mistress pinned up the hem. She couldn't help wrinkling her nose in distaste.

If there was anything negative about playing Maggie in *Cat on a Hot Rin Roof*, Bess thought, this was it.

This was what she would wear for the whole play, a slinky, white full slip.

She had been so doubtful about getting the part, she hadn't given the costume a second thought. How can I walk around half-naked in front of an audience, she thought frantically.

"So, how's the costume feel?"

Startled, Bess looked up and saw Daphne's reflection staring back at her in the mirror.

"Ooops," Daphne said. A smile slid across her face. "Sorry I asked," she went on. "Obviously, not too good."

"The seams need to be let out a bit," Amanda murmured to herself but out loud.

Before Bess could say anything, Daphne leaned forward and whispered in her ear.

"You do realize you're—uh—just a bit too *plump* to play Maggie."

Instantly, Bess's face felt aflame. She would have given anything for a sweatshirt or a jacket or even a blanket to throw over herself.

"That slip would have looked much better

on me," Daphne continued. "And Amanda'd be taking it *in*, not letting it *out*. Just don't say I didn't warn you," she said as she stalked off.

Amanda looked as startled as Bess by Daphne's nasty remarks. "Now, that Daphne Gillman knows how to play a cat," she commented.

Tears were stinging Bess's eyes. She tried to fight them back, but several slid down her cheeks. "Don't worry," Amanda said, patting Bess on the shoulder. "No one will notice your weight. They'll just be paying attention to you and the play. Besides, there's not a thing wrong with your weight."

Bess nodded and smiled her thanks as Amanda walked away, but the girl's kind words only made things worse. Even she had mentioned Bess's weight problem.

A part of Bess wanted to believe that Daphne was just being mean—that she was still upset she hadn't gotten the part herself. But another part of her, the part that was looking at her reflection, thought something else.

She was too fat to play Maggie!

As Nancy left the campus post office, she put the letter back in the envelope. The return address was Los Angeles, California, and the letter was from Judd. It was short, sweet, to the point, and no surprise. He was sorry they hadn't had more time together. He missed the magic they had. He missed kissing her. But they had to move on.

"Move on," Nancy muttered, heading for the athletic fields for her appointment with Gary. "That's what I'd planned on doing . . . with you!" She sighed and put the letter in her pocket.

After her intense and emotional relationships with Ned and Jake, Nancy had really been looking forward to something sweet and fun. Judd had seemed perfect. From the beginning she had been drawn to his blue eyes, his soft voice that was an intimate surprise, and to his strength, the strength that had led him to expose his track coach as a drug pusher.

As disappointed as she was, Nancy had to admit that there was something nice about being on her own again. It reminded her of how she'd felt when she first arrived on campus—ready to find out about herself and what she wanted.

When Nancy reached the gates to the tennis center, she saw Gary sitting on the ground surrounded by his photo equipment. The cup of coffee clutched in his hand had tipped and spilled into the grass. He was resting his head against the wire mesh of the fence, his jaw open, sound asleep.

Behind him, the sounds of the neon yellow balls being batted back and forth across the courts and the coaches' shouting out orders filled the air.

Nancy reached down to shake Gary's shoulder. "Good morning," she said brightly.

"Sorry," Gary mumbled, scrambling to his feet.

"Still not getting any sleep?"

Gary rubbed his eyes. "Trevor was at it again all night."

Nancy lifted her eyebrows. "Maybe you should consider filing a complaint with the university if he won't do anything about it."

Gary shrugged. "I'll think about it."

"You know, my roommate wasn't so hot at first either," Nancy admitted. "She used to borrow things from me without asking, and stay up late partying, and just kind of crowd me in general, not respecting my privacy and stuff."

"What did you do?" Gary asked.

"Talked it out, confronted her about it," Nancy replied. "She's still not perfect, but she's a lot better. Even if we're not the best friends in the world, we're totally friendly and supportive. We've gotten used to each other's lifestyle."

Gary shook his head. "I wish I had the chance to talk to him. When he's not at his desk, blasting music on his Walkman, he's rushing out to organic chemistry, or statistics, or some premed club or other. I doubt we've said more than three or four sentences in a row to each other since the beginning of the semester."

"Maybe it's time to start thinking of moving out," Nancy suggested.

"Maybe," Gary said. But Nancy could tell he wasn't serious about it. Gary was such a laid-back guy—he'd probably just go on putting up with Trevor and his all-nighters.

Nancy noticed that something had caught Gary's eye. She followed his gaze through the gates. The players were coming off the courts, and Mara Lindon was in the lead. She was slim and tall, with long brown hair swept in a high ponytail off a pretty face.

Nancy could easily see why Gary had paid attention to Mara during freshman orientation. She would stand out in any crowd. Not only was she attractive, but she exuded a healthy, athletic glow. No wonder she and George were friends—they were both really into athletics.

She's the perfect image for the whole Women in Athletics project, Nancy thought.

"Ready, Gary?" Nancy asked. "This is an important shot."

But Gary already had his camera out and aimed at the girl moving toward them. "I'm way ahead of you, Nance," he mumbled. "I just wish I'd gotten my beauty sleep."

* * *

"Don't American reporters use notebooks?" Nadia asked, grinning wryly.

Jake's smile faded. He blushed fiercely as he added another scribbled-on Java Joe's menu to his stack. He must have used ten or fifteen by now, filling the backs of them with Nadia's life story. The two of them sat for so long that by now the lunchtime crowd was starting to pour into the coffee shop.

Jake cleared his throat. "I forgot my notebook," he mumbled.

Nadia clucked, wagging a finger. "Not very professional."

Yeah, no kidding, he chided himself. But who would have thought I was going to interview the most interesting—and drop-dead beautiful—woman on the face of the planet?

Jake looked her full in the face and drank her in, her mysterious dark eyes, the chiseled grace of her face. He wanted to believe he hadn't been this head over heels about anybody before. And he probably hadn't been— except about Nancy.

Nancy was out of his life now, he reminded himself. At least in the head-over-heels department.

"Believe it or not, this isn't my first assignment," Jake said.

Nadia shrugged. "Maybe it's the American way, to be unprepared."

The comment stung his professional reporter

ego. "No, it's not the American way," he protested.

"Your way, then."

"Let's just say I wasn't expecting to have to work so hard," he said, and gave her a winning smile.

Now it was Nadia's turn to blush. The air, which thrummed with magnetic attraction from the moment they had met, now seemed to crackle with electricity. Jake was positive he wasn't the only one aware of the high voltage.

"You know what they say in Russia?" Nadia asked in her silky, sexy accent. "Nothing's worthwhile that isn't hard."

"They say that in Russia, do they?" Jake queried, holding back a smile.

Nadia sat back, her hands folded across her stomach, and gave Jake an unabashed stare. "So, was *this* worthwhile?"

Jake raised an eyebrow. "It was interesting hearing about your father's newspaper," he teased.

"Was it?" she replied coolly. "Anything else?"

Jake could feel the tug of a grin. *"You're* moderately interesting."

"Moderately?" Nadia said, playing up the disappointment. She puckered her sumptuous lips and fingered the scarf at her neck, as if she were thinking that over. "Is there anything else that I could tell you to make me more than moderately interesting?"

Jake nibbled on the end of his pencil. There was really only one question he'd wanted to ask her since he'd sat down. But he'd been saving it—or was that burying it? To ask the subject of an interview out was definitely a journalistic no-no. But he was already guilty of one faux pas—forgetting a notebook, so what the heck.

He picked up his pen again. "I'm sure the Wilder students will be dying to know if you have someone waiting for you in Russia."

"Oh, really?" Nadia laughed out loud. "May I ask, is this on the record?"

"Of course, definitely," Jake replied, all business.

"In that case, the answer is no. Just as Russia is now free from the Communists, I am now free from men. I am a free woman."

Jake smiled nervously. "That's a pretty strong statement. What about *off* the record?"

Nadia's return smile was warm. "Still, I say no boyfriend."

"Well," Jake said, folding up the menus, "I think I have everything I need—except one thing. I was wondering if you'd like some more off-the-record conversation, over dinner sometime?"

Nadia's smile turned demure and catlike.

Jake, sure he was about to be turned down,

felt a strong pang of regret. You blew it, he chided himself.

For the last hour Nadia had been full of surprises, and they didn't end there.

"I would like that very much," she said finally.

"Good," Jake said, grinning. "I'll call you."

At that, they both stood abruptly. Nadia fastened her scarf around her neck and wrapped herself in a black wool cape. Jake began to gather his things, reluctant to say goodbye.

Suddenly their eyes met across the table. "What direction are you headed?" each of them asked at the same time. Then they both broke up, laughing.

Jake could feel his face flush. He held out his hand. "You first." Nadia looked at her watch and shrugged. "Back to my room, I suppose. I don't have classes until Monday morning, but I have hard work ahead of me, getting to know my new suitemates."

"Are they treating you well?" Jake asked.

Nadia nodded earnestly. "Oh, yes, they're wonderful. I love them. Especially my new roommate."

"Good," Jake said. "Maybe I can talk to them, too."

Nadia looked at him surprised.

"To round out my article," Jake explained quickly. "What it's like to live with a Russian transfer student with such a colorful background."

"Oh," Nadia said.

Another loud silence.

"Then would you mind if I walked you over?" Jake asked.

"I was hoping you would," Nadia replied, visibly relieved. "I just arrived last night, and though I could find my way here, I do not know if I can find my way back."

As Jake followed her out the door, he could feel his heart leap a little. Even after Nick's pep talk, he hadn't believed it could happen. But it had, he realized. This morning another woman had actually made him forget about Nancy Drew.

CHAPTER 5

At lunchtime Java Joe's was teeming with activity. The line at the counter snaked out the door. Circled around a small table, George, Nancy, and Bess had to lean their heads together just to hear.

"Will and I haven't had the easiest couple of weeks," George said, explaining to her friends why she wanted to do something special for her boyfriend. "Especially since we weren't sure if the relationship was going to make it."

"Well, you two have weathered a pretty scary storm," Nancy said.

"Exactly." George smiled. "Which is why I'm planning a big romantic evening for us."

"Oh, that's so sweet," Bess said. Her eyes were focused on the chocolate cake she had gotten to go with her mocha latte. George

48

wasn't sure if Bess was talking about her romantic evening with Will or her dessert.

"Well, I may have a scoop abut a budding romance," Nancy said, her eyes twinkling.

"Who?" Bess asked. "Someone in your suite?"

"Someone George knows," Nancy said. "Mara Lindon, the tennis player."

"Mara?" George asked. "Who's she going out with?"

"Well, Gary Friedman—you know the photographer at the paper—came with me this morning when I interviewed her for the paper," Nancy said. "And sparks seemed to fly between them. He got up the nerve to ask her out and they're doing something together tonight."

"That's great," George said enthusiastically. "Gary seems like such a nice guy and Mara really deserves someone like that now."

"What do you mean?" Bess asked.

"Well, Mara's old boyfriend was a complete jerk," George told them, lowering her voice as much as she could and still be heard in the crowded coffee shop. "His name is Sean Masters and he was totally jealous and controlling. He was awful to Mara, and no one could figure out why she kept seeing him. But she told me that she recently broke up with Sean."

"Good timing, then," Nancy said. "At least for Gary."

"Sounds like it," George agreed.

"Yeah," Bess said, pushing her chocolate cake to the other side of the table. "Too sweet."

George stared at her cousin. "Are you talking about Gary and Mara or the cake, Bess?"

"What?" Bess asked guiltily.

George pointed to the cake.

"Aren't you going to eat that?" Nancy chimed in. "A few minutes ago you were telling us how delicious it looked."

"I know," Bess admitted. "But that was a few minutes ago. I just remembered I'm on a diet." She dropped her chin in her hand, disappointed.

George gave her cousin a quick glance.

This wasn't the first time that Bess had seemed overly concerned about her appearance and her weight. But George didn't want to jump to any conclusions. Maybe Bess was just being more careful now that she was a star.

When she glanced at Nancy, George could see the same concern for Bess mirrored in her friend's eyes. But Nancy let the subject drop, too.

"So guess what?" she said instead. "I've decided to throw a surprise party for my father."

"You threw a great surprise party for Jake," George said. "Not to bring up any bad memories," she added quickly.

"No, it's true." Nancy laughed. "And planning that party was a lot of fun. So I should be able to pull off another one."

"It sounds like a great idea," George said.

"He'll love it," Bess agreed. "And it should help shrink the distance between you guys."

"I hope so," Nancy said wistfully. "I really want it to be perfect."

"Have you called Avery yet to talk to her about it?" George asked.

"Well," Nancy said, her eyes cast down at her coffee cup. "Not exactly . . ."

George was hoping that Nancy would be able to straighten things out with her father *and* with Avery. But from Nancy's expression, it was obvious that Nancy wasn't quite ready to patch things up with Avery.

George took a long sip of her spring water and gazed out the window at the quad. Suddenly she saw Jake Collins walk by with a dark-haired woman George had never seen before.

Her eyes followed them, trying to see who Jake's mystery woman was, but their heads were bent so close together that George couldn't get a good look at her face. All she could see was dark, flowing hair and a bright red scarf tied around the woman's neck.

George shot a quick glance at Nancy, but Nancy and Bess had started chatting again, and Nancy hadn't noticed Jake or his companion. George knew that Nancy had said she was over

Jake, but still . . . it was always hard to see an old boyfriend with someone new—especially someone as beautiful as this girl appeared to be.

George almost pointed Jake out to Nancy, but she changed her mind. *Nancy has enough to worry about with her dad and Avery,* George decided, taking another sip of water. For now, George would keep what she had seen to herself.

As Jake led Nadia through the Walk, a wide path that cut across campus, he took a deep breath and tried to pull himself together. His heart was racing and his head was starting to pound.

Nadia had just finished telling him about the day her father was released from the work camp in Siberia, and how he was hailed as a hero in Moscow. And how, together with his family, he had started the newspaper called *Liberation.*

Is there anything not *fascinating about this woman?* Jake asked himself.

"What a perfect day for me to come to Wilder," Nadia said, clutching her cape around her. Her eyes glinted with energy and exhilaration as she took in the bright sunshine. "The light is so fiery and intense."

Just like you, Jake thought. For him, walking next to Nadia was like being in close proximity to a power plant. The air around her vibrated with energy.

Am I falling in love with her already? he wondered. He looked at his watch. If he had fallen in love, it was in record time. It would take longer to write his article for the *Times*.

Suddenly Nadia stopped and glanced around, staring hard at the buildings.

"You're not much of a tour guide," she scolded him good-naturedly.

Jake cleared his throat. "Sorry, I guess I have something on my mind."

"Something good or something bad?"

"Good—I hope," Jake said meaningfully. "Anyway, that's Holliston Stadium over there." He pointed to the high circular wall and Grecian columns on his right. "That's where the football team plays."

Nadia craned her neck and nodded her approval. "I don't know anything about football, but I like the school colors, maroon and white. The colors of blood and victory."

Jake cocked his head. Blood and victory? He shook his head at the exotic ideas that came out of her mouth, that rolled off her tongue. . . .

Suddenly, without warning, she bolted off the path and, waving her arms, kicked through a pile of fallen leaves, sending a red and yellow shower upward. "I just *love* this time of year!" she cried.

Jake smiled at her exuberance.

"In Moscow, it goes from summer to winter in one day," Nadia went on. "It's like an oven—then, boom! it's like the North Pole. Here in America you get so many more seasons. So much variety, and it is all so beautiful."

Not half as beautiful as you, Jake thought.

"I think my dorm is that way," Nadia said. She nudged Jake, with her shoulder, toward a group of dorm buildings. It was an all too familiar sight to Jake.

He slowed his stride. "Nadia, which dorm do you live in?"

"That one."

Jake's eyes followed her finger as she pointed. He swallowed hard. "Thayer Hall?"

Nadia nodded. "Thayer. Is Thayer a name?"

"Maybe he was a past president of the university," Jake guessed. "Or maybe he was just some rich guy who donated the building."

As they headed toward Thayer Hall, Jake's mind was calculating the odds of Nadia's being Stephanie's replacement in suite 301. He knew that Stephanie had just gotten married and that it was one of the strangest turns of events in the history of the planet. It would only be fitting—maddeningly fitting—that the one girl who seemed to be the answer to his hopes and dreams was the one who . . .

"Is there anything wrong?" Nadia asked, breaking into his thoughts.

"Why?" Jake demanded nervously.

"Because I can tell. I can feel something is wrong."

Jake gazed at Nadia, at her nose and cheeks rouged by the chill, her porcelain skin—the most beautiful face he'd ever seen.

"Let me ask you something, Nadia," he started.

Nadia's face broke into a sly grin.

"On or off the record?" she asked.

"Definitely on," Jake said. "Who is your new roommate?"

Even before Nadia said, "Casey Fontaine," Jake was nodding and saying, "Yep." It had to be. It was just his luck. He groaned. "You live in suite three-oh-one."

"Why so disappointed?" she asked, obviously confused. "The girls there are wonderful. They're interesting, they're helpful, and—"

"I know," Jake interrupted.

Nadia eyed him. "You know? How would you know?"

He waved a hand in the air helplessly. "Nancy Drew is my old girlfriend."

"Ah," Nadia said, nodding. "I see the dilemma." Her face darkened for a minute. But then she smiled and shrugged. "That is life, no?"

"What is?" Jake asked. Was this to be the end of it, before it really began?

"Nancy will have to understand if we go out to dinner together."

Relieved, Jake breathed.

"Unless *you* will feel too awkward," Nadia added.

Jake quickly shook his head. "It may be a little uncomfortable, but that is life, no?" he said, mimicking Nadia's accent.

They both erupted in laughter.

"You agree with my philosophy," Nadia said.

"What philosophy is that?"

"That you only live once," she replied soberly.

Jake nodded. "I like that philosophy. How about tomorrow night?"

"So, you'll definitely be able to make it?" Nancy asked, cradling the phone against her shoulder. "Great." She smiled, crossing another name off the list on her desk. "And remember, don't tell him a thing!"

Nancy hung up the phone and leaned back in her chair. Everything was coming together perfectly, and she couldn't keep from laughing to herself with excitement.

"You sound pretty happy with yourself," Kara said from across the room. Nancy's roommate was lounging on her bed, flipping through a stack of notes from her calculus class. "Let's have the party update."

"What can I say?" Nancy grinned, turning around in her chair. "Next Friday night is going to be the best party ever."

"And the whole thing is a surprise, right?" Kara asked. "At your dad's house?"

"Yep," Nancy said. "I've already called the best caterer in River Heights—for hors d'oeuvres and desserts. And a great DJ who has this amazing collection of music. There will be cool contemporary stuff, but a lot of older stuff, too, for Dad's friends."

"I guess they should be allowed to enjoy themselves." Kara grinned. "I bet it will be really fun. You just have to figure out how you're going to do the magic."

"What magic?" Nancy asked.

"The magic that gets hundreds of people into your house without your father noticing." Kara arched her brow.

"Oh, yes. Well, those people come in while we're out," Nancy explained. "I'll be taking Dad to an early dinner—just for the two of us. And he'll think that was the whole plan. Then, when we get back—"

"Surprise City." Kara nodded. "Sounds great."

"Now I just need to talk to Hannah." Nancy sighed as she reached for the phone again. The last time Nancy had tried to call her housekeeper to arrange all of the party plans, her dad had answered the phone. Nancy had ended up pretending she'd called for something else. She knew her excuse had probably sounded ridiculous. She just hoped it wouldn't make her father suspicious that something was up.

Nancy dialed her old number again.

"Drew residence," a familiar voice answered.

"Oh, good, Hannah, it's you!" Nancy cried. "Quick, don't say anything about its being me on the phone. I have to talk to you about something secret."

There was just a second's pause before Hannah replied.

"Oh, yes, Gladys, I can get the name of that book for you. Let me just switch phones to my room so I won't bother Mr. Drew here in the den."

Nancy chuckled. Hannah was a smooth operator. It must have been all those years of living with Nancy and her dad.

Moments later, after hanging up the den phone, Hannah was back on the line.

"So what's the secret?" Hannah asked. "Besides you. You haven't been calling much lately."

Nancy winced. Obviously, even Hannah had sensed the tension between Nancy, Carson, and Avery the last time Nancy was home. But that would all be in the past after Nancy gave her father this party.

"I know," Nancy said. "But I'm calling now for something really important. It's Dad's birthday next week, and I've got something great planned. I've called a bunch of Dad's friends, and they're all going to come over next Friday night for a surprise party. I'll need your help setting things up and getting Dad out of the way."

"Oh, Nancy," Hannah said, sounding troubled. "A surprise party? And you've already done so much work. Oh, but that would have been wonderful."

"Would have been?" Nancy repeated, her stomach sinking. "What do you mean?"

"Well, Nancy, you should have called me sooner, or asked Avery," Hannah explained.

"What's Avery got to do with it?" Nancy asked, a little more sharply than she wished. "I mean, she's invited, of course."

"Of course," Hannah agreed. "But that's not the problem. You see Avery's already made some birthday arrangements for your father and herself. I believe they're going to a lovely little bed-and-breakfast for the weekend—by a lake up north."

Nancy almost dropped the phone. Hannah was still talking, but Nancy wasn't hearing anymore. She felt completely numb. She could see Kara looking at her worriedly.

Avery's already made some birthday arrangements for your father and herself . . .

Suddenly Nancy remembered when her father had told her about his new girlfriend. It had been another phone conversation that had left Nancy feeling shocked and unsure.

"Nancy," Hannah was saying. "Avery's arrangements were made a while ago, but I'm sure if you spoke to her—"

"No, no," Nancy interrupted. "It's no problem," she continued mechanically. "I'll just drop the whole thing."

But the truth was, there was a huge problem—and her name was Avery Fallon.

Avery was a lawyer, just like Nancy's dad. Nancy knew her dad wanted her to like Avery, but she didn't. And now Avery had made plans for Carson's birthday without consulting her. It was just further proof that Avery didn't like Nancy. She certainly didn't care about Nancy's feelings.

Nancy was livid by the time she hung up.

"How could she even *think* of making plans for him without asking me?" she muttered.

Nancy looked at the list of people she'd already called—and thought of calling them all back. Then she thought of all the things she had to cancel.

All the things that wouldn't happen.

As she picked up the phone again, Nancy had to bite her lip to keep from crying.

Avery had sabotaged her plans for setting things right with her dad.

CHAPTER 6

Nancy tossed and turned in bed. She had been trying to fall asleep for six hours—it felt like six days—but every time she closed her eyes, the thoughts that rushed into her head made her open them again. She couldn't stop thinking about all the men she seemed to have lost over the last few months: Ned, Jake, Judd. Now she was afraid she was losing her father, too.

Finally Nancy decided to give up on trying to sleep. She had to meet Gary soon, anyway, to interview the women's rugby team. Kara's steady breathing kept Nancy company while she quietly pulled open one of her drawers and withdrew a sweater. Her jeans were on her chair. She dressed and slipped soundlessly from the room.

Outside, the morning air was brittle and cold. Nancy hurried to the newspaper office. It

61

was deathly quiet as she unlocked the door. Inside, there was no sign of Gary.

"Gary? Don't tell me I rushed over here for nothing," she said out loud.

"Over here." The voice sounded hoarse. It came from the lounge area of the office, which sported a coffee machine, a "pillow pit," and a secondhand couch. Gary was stretched out on the pillows. He had on jeans, a rumpled sweater, and a T-shirt wrapped around his head.

" 'Morning," he said sleepily.

"Have you been here all night?" Nancy asked.

Gary nodded.

"Trevor again?"

Gary groaned in response.

"You've got to do something about this," Nancy insisted. "Your room and board includes the cost of a bed, you know."

"Hey, that's it." Gary held up a finger, pretending something had just dawned on him. "My parents paid extra for a psycho insomniac roommate just to get me back for all my childhood crimes."

Rolling her eyes, Nancy collapsed on the couch. "Well, if it makes you feel any better, I didn't get much sleep myself last night."

Gary propped himself up on an elbow. "Why not?"

She filled him in on what had happened to her plans for a surprise party.

"That's too bad," Gary said sympathetically. "It must be hard to share your dad after so many years of there being just the two of you."

"It is," Nancy confessed. To her surprise she felt much better. Gary was a good listener, and he was the first person she'd talked to about the situation who hadn't pointed out that her dad had a right to his own life. Instead he'd just acknowledged that her dad's having a girlfriend was a big change for everyone.

"Thanks for listening," Nancy said. "So, how was your date with Mara?"

"Great!" he said happily. "She's really nice, and I think she had a good time, too."

"Good." Nancy checked her watch. "Oops. It's getting late. You can give me the details on the way over, but we'd better catch the rugby team before they get into a scrum or something."

Gary rose to his feet, rubbed his eyes, and declared himself ready.

"So where'd you two go?" Nancy started to ask. But Gary never answered, for as they reached the *Wilder Times* door, a dark silhouette loomed outside the pane of frosted glass.

"Are you expecting someone?" Nancy whispered.

Gary shook his head as a loud, forceful knock rattled the door. Tentatively, Nancy opened it.

Standing like a mountain was an enormous guy with wide shoulders and arms the size of Nancy's thighs. Nancy vaguely remembered seeing him on the football team. His face wore a furious expression.

"You're history!" he snarled, and shoved Gary about five feet backward. "I saw you with Mara last night!" The guy pointed a finger at Gary and slowly started toward him.

Nancy saw Gary swallow hard. "I'm sorry . . ." he managed to say. "I mean, I'm *not* sorry. You don't own her, Sean."

His face beet red, Sean reached for Gary's neck with his right hand and clutched his shoulder with his left.

Nancy screamed as Sean squeezed his right hand tight around Gary's throat.

"Hey! Break it up!" She lunged at Sean's back. Moving him was as impossible as moving a parked car, but he did let go of Gary.

"Leave my girlfriend alone, you twerp!" Sean shouted.

"Not your girlfriend . . . anymore," Gary croaked. "It's a free country."

"I'm calling campus police!" Nancy cried,

and ran to a phone. Gary sank to the floor, holding his neck with both hands.

"If I see you within ten feet of Mara," the football player threatened him, "I'll do a lot worse to you!" He turned around like a tornado and stormed out of the office.

Nancy sprinted over to Gary and knelt beside him. "Are you okay? Let me see your neck."

Gary waved her away. "I'm fine," he said hoarsely.

Nancy looked back over her shoulder. "I take it that's Sean Masters we just met."

"Yep." Gary rolled his eyes as he pushed himself up the wall to his feet. "Starting defensive tackle, resident thug—"

"And Mara Lindon's ex-boyfriend," Nancy finished. "Though he hasn't taken very well to being the ex, has he?"

"Doesn't appear that way," Gary agreed, rubbing his neck. "He's been following her around ever since she told him to take a hike."

"That's called stalking, Gary," said Nancy.

"She warned me about this last night."

"Really?" Nancy was worried.

Gary nodded. "Good thing he stopped before he strangled me," he said with a rueful grin. "I'd like to live long enough to take her out again."

Nancy wasn't smiling at his lame joke. She lifted his chin and gently examined his neck.

"It looks okay," she said. "But maybe we should still head over to campus police and file a complaint."

Gary shook his head. "I'm not ready to do that. I'll think about it."

"Go with Mara and she can file a complaint at the same time." Gary just shook his head.

"Well, be careful if you do go out with Mara again," she warned him. "Sean seemed pretty irate. He'll probably come after you again."

Gary nodded. "Don't worry, Nance. I'll be careful. I value my life, you know."

"So you'll get help if you need it?" Nancy asked.

Rubbing his neck, Gary smiled. "You mean, like the National Guard?"

"I'm serious, Gary," she said. "A guy with violent tendencies like that can't be taken lightly."

"Sure. I'll get help if I think I need it," Gary promised. "In the meantime, which way to the rugby fields?" he added with a wink. "You'd better get all the pictures you can out of me before it's too late."

As the bells in the campus clock tower chimed nine o'clock, George slowed her stride. She waited for a tall, muscular girl to catch up to her. Like George, the girl was wearing black running tights, a windbreaker, and gloves to keep her hands warm.

"Hey, Mara," George said.

Mara smiled. "Ready for our run?"

George nodded.

"How about an easy five?" Mara asked. "I have tennis practice later."

"Sure." Five miles means about forty minutes, George calculated. Which should be long enough to get all the information I need.

Although George was looking forward to the run with Mara, she did have an ulterior motive: Nancy and Bess had entrusted her with the all-important task of finding out how Mara's date with Gary went. They'd told her she couldn't return until she had all the juicy details.

George and Mara took off, with George setting a brisk pace. They were about the same height and build, so they easily fell into a steady, rhythmic stride, pumping their arms together, totally in sync.

They turned a bend and entered the gravel path that circled the lake.

"So, do you like Wilder?" George asked Mara. Even though she and Mara had hung out together before, George realized she didn't know much about her.

Mara nodded. "Yes, a lot," she started. "But it took me a while to get settled. The first month wasn't exactly the best time of my life. I made some really bizarre choices. Like taking three upper-level courses at once and going out with that creep Sean Masters." She glanced at George. "Do you know Sean?"

"Seen him around campus," George said between breaths. "He's, uh . . . big."

Mara let out a laugh. "Let's just say the size of his brain is inversely proportional to the size of his gargantuan body. My experience with him was enough to shake my faith in the entire male species. Anyway, it's over. Thank goodness."

A pair of male runners were coming the other way. As they passed, both guys waved.

"*They* were cute," George commented.

Mara flashed her a grin. "Don't you have a boyfriend?"

"And *he's* cute, too," George replied, laughing.

"Well, I'm swearing off jocks," Mara declared. "All Sean could talk about or think about was football. And he was so jealous it was beyond belief. Once, he yelled at me for winking at the library clerk at the Rock. Can you believe it, the *library* clerk? That man is in his fifties!"

George and Mara dissolved in laughter and slowed to a stop. They bent over, hands on knees.

Once George got her breath back, she said,

"So, I heard a rumor that you had a big date last night."

"I went out with Gary Friedman. He doesn't have an athletic bone in his body."

"I know him," George said. "He's nice—and cute, too."

Mara looked at her. "He *is* cute, in a kind of clean-cut, nerdy way. After we had dinner, he took me to his darkroom and showed me how he develops his pictures."

"Darkroom?" George couldn't resist teasing Mara.

Though Mara was red from the running, George noticed that her face had deepened another shade or two.

"Don't worry." Mara grinned. "I'm not about to jump right into another hot-and-heavy relationship. But let's just say that Gary has begun to restore my faith in guys. Last night he helped me remember how well some guys can treat girls. . . . Shall we?" Mara asked, starting to run again.

George fell into step beside her, glad that Mara had had a good time the night before. And wait till Bess and Nancy heard that Gary had taken Mara to his darkroom.

When Bess finally got back to her dorm room Saturday afternoon, she felt as if she were about to faint. She'd tried to study all day, but she'd spent most of her time drifting in and out of sleep. And when she wasn't sleeping, she couldn't concentrate on her schoolwork.

All she could think about was what Daphne had said to her in the costume room: "You're too plump to be Maggie."

What if the audience thought she was too fat, too? Bess thought. Then they'd spend the whole time looking at her in her costume and thinking about how heavy she was instead of paying attention to her acting. That would ruin the whole play.

But Professor Glasseburg was a professional. She would never have cast me if she thought there was any danger of that, right? Bess reasoned.

She shrugged off her backpack and turned it over onto her bed. A few bags of potato chips and packages of cookies spilled out. As Bess sat down on the bed, her head was spinning. Was she dizzy because she was tense, or was it because she hadn't eaten anything all day?

Not that she hadn't bought food, Bess thought, looking at the collection of junk she'd brought home. But at least she'd only bought it. She had stopped herself before she actually ate it.

Bess reached down and pulled a shoe box out from under her bed. Inside was a growing collection of snacks and candy bars. Bess swept everything off her bed into the shoe box.

As she looked at a chocolate bar lying on top, she felt a wave of hunger. Before she even realized what she was doing, she'd opened the candy bar and was halfway done with it.

No! her mind screamed at her. You've tried so hard to be good all day, and now you're ruining it!

Somehow Bess couldn't stop herself. Within minutes, she'd finished the candy bar and two bags of chips. She was reaching for a package of cookies when she heard someone at the door.

Quickly Bess shoved the box of food back under her bed. She looked up just as the door swung open. Her roommate, Leslie King, entered in a huff.

"Leslie?" Bess managed to gulp out, swallowing the last mouthful of chips.

"Hi, Bess," Leslie said, tossing her book bag onto her bed. "I spent the whole afternoon in the library." Leslie checked her watch. "But I came back because Nathan wants to take me out to dinner."

"Dinner?" Bess echoed numbly.

At that moment Bess couldn't imagine eating dinner—or anything else for that matter. Now that Leslie had interrupted her food orgy, Bess was shocked at what she'd done to herself. It was disgusting how she'd just lost total control.

"And so Nathan said he wanted to make up for the fight we had last week by taking me out tonight," Leslie was saying. "What do you think, Bess?"

"What?" Bess asked, dazed. "Tonight? That sounds nice."

"I guess," Leslie said as she began brushing out her hair.

Leslie went on talking about the disagreement between herself and her boyfriend, Nathan Kress, but Bess barely heard her. Had she seen her chowing down like a pig? Bess wiped her mouth, wondering if there were potato chip crumbs all over her face.

Suddenly Leslie stopped talking and peered curiously at Bess. "Do you need some lip balm?"

"Uh, thanks," Bess said. Her face flushed as Leslie handed her a small tube. "My lips are really sore."

"So, anyway," Leslie went on, "Nathan started telling me all about this new restaurant he's heard about—"

Bess couldn't stop thinking about all the junk she had just eaten. What's going to happen when I go to rehearsal on Monday? she wondered. There's no way I'm going to fit into that slip. Not after the binge I just had.

"And I told him no way was I interested in going to some disgusting greasy diner across town," Leslie was still chatting.

"Of course not," Bess managed. She'd made up her mind.

She'd skip dinner tonight, and breakfast tomorrow. That was the only way to make sure that her slip would fit on Monday.

in another love.

"And I told him no way was I interested in going to some ridiculous fancy dinner across town," Nadia was still chatting.

"Of course not," Tina assured. She'd made up her mind.

She'd talk to the chairman about it tomorrow. That was the only way to make sure that her date would be out of her life.

CHAPTER 7

You know what the best part of dinner was?" Jake asked.

Nadia stopped and lifted her face. Her eyes—as dark and endless as the night around her—were deeply serious.

She and Jake were standing on the sidewalk outside Blake's Place, the best hamburger joint in Weston. They'd had burgers, fries, and milk shakes, as American a meal as Jake could come up with, as per Nadia's request.

"The best part was being able to look at you all evening," Jake finished the thought.

The comment seemed to surprise them both. Not that it wasn't what they were both thinking. After all, they'd spent their dinner laughing and listening to each other's stories. Jake told her about some of the articles he'd written, especially the one about college hate crimes, which had been picked up by a major

Chicago paper. Meanwhile Nadia continued to amaze him with stories about her life back home.

Jake loved watching Nadia's gestures and facial expressions. Actually, he loved every detail of her. When she was making an important point, her arms flailed about and her dark eyes flashed with excitement.

"I could listen to you all night," she said suddenly.

Which was just what Jake was going to say. Before Nadia beat him to it.

"Does the evening have to end now?" he asked. "It's—" he looked at his watch "—only nine o'clock. And the night's been perfect so far."

"It has been perfect. I wish it would not end." Nadia's smile melted Jake's heart. As they stood to leave, Jake draped Nadia's cape around her shoulders. He wished he didn't have to let her go. "It has been perfect," she repeated as they stepped outside. Then her expression darkened.

"Nadia?" Jake asked. "What's wrong?"

Nadia bit her lip and wound a strand of hair around her finger. "Nancy," she murmured. "I was to tell her I was seeing you tonight because I wanted to be honest with her. But I did not have the chance. I haven't seen her all day. I don't want to upset her or come between you two."

Jake shook his head. "Nancy's completely over me," he stated. "And I . . . well, let's put it this way. I had strong feelings for her once, but you've made it a lot easier to forget about her."

Nadia stared intently at him, obviously deciding whether to believe him. Jake sucked in his breath. Nancy had barely crossed his mind till now.

Since he'd met Nadia, he had let go and had barely even thought about Nancy Drew.

"Well, that *is* good news," Nadia said softly. "I was worried your heart was somewhere else."

Jake leveled a steady gaze at Nadia. The pull between them was too strong to resist. He stepped toward her and cupped Nadia's face in his hands. His lips sought hers. As they came together, Jake inhaled the unusual scent she wore. He wanted to keep this moment locked in his mind forever.

Nadia pulled his face toward hers. Her touch was soft but firm and determined. And the kiss was as passionate as anything Jake had ever felt—electric—and filled with all the emotions and thoughts and stories they'd shared in the last twenty-four hours, and all the words they hadn't yet said.

"Wow," Jake said as they pulled apart. Around them the busy street was a blur.

Nadia turned away shyly, but she was smiling.

"I've never felt such a close connection so quickly," Jake said as they started walking again. Nadia stopped and pressed a finger to his lips. "Shh," she said. "It is too nice for words now."

True, Jake realized, glad that she had stopped him. Maybe it was a Russian thing— or maybe it was just a Nadia thing—to enjoy a moment without spoiling it with words.

A few minutes later Jake realized that they weren't far from Club Z. He turned to Nadia. "Want to go dancing? I know a club where they play great music."

"I love to dance!" Nadia exclaimed. "Which way?"

Jake quickly led her in the direction of Club Z. As they headed inside the crowded dance club, Jake realized that only one thing stood between him and total bliss: the fact that Nancy lived across the hall from Nadia.

I loved Nancy once, Jake reminded himself. But she pushed me away. The breakup was her choice. And now it's my turn to make a choice. . . .

"So, are you still sorry?" George whispered into Will's ear. The two of them were doing a slow dance at Club Z, a lingering spiral in the middle of the dance floor.

A live out-of-town band called Saturnine was onstage, awash in the glow from purple spotlights. Other couples spun around George and Will as the band kicked up the beat.

Will tightened his grip. "I'm sorry I haven't been as understanding as I could have been," he said, "but I'm not sorry the whole thing came up. I think I love you even more than I did before."

George shut her eyes and lost herself in the music and the feeling of being held in Will's strong, caring arms.

Abruptly, an arm clamped down on George's shoulder. "Hey!" she cried as someone spun her around.

"Where's Mara?" a deep voice growled.

Uh-oh, George thought as she looked up at the huge, muscular guy who blocked her view. She'd heard about Nancy and Gary's run-in with Sean Masters, and George had a feeling she was about to get a firsthand understanding of what it had been like.

"You must be Sean," George said wryly.

"Where is she?" he demanded.

Just then Will stepped between them. "You know this guy?" he asked George.

Sensing trouble, some of the other dancers on the floor had stopped to watch.

"I know *of* him," George said. "He's Mara's *ex*-boyfriend."

"Look, I know you and Mara are friends. I

saw you two running together this morning," Sean went on.

George folded her arms across her chest and stared at him in disbelief. "Were you actually spying on us? I guess Mara was right about you being a jealous psycho."

Sean took a step toward George, a menacing expression on his face. A small gasp rose from the crowd.

"Watch out, buddy," Will warned, glowering at him. They stood toe to toe, glaring at each other.

"You have anything to say to George, you say it to me," Will demanded.

Will was tall and muscular, and a terrific athlete, but next to Sean he looked like a shrimp.

"Forget it, Will," George said, tugging on his arm. "It isn't worth it, fighting this guy. In fact, he isn't worth anything."

At her remark, George saw Sean's face flush with anger. His fists closed and opened. "I'm going to ask you one more time: Where's Mara?"

George stared at him. There was no way she was going to tell this animal that Mara had said she might be going out with Gary again tonight.

Someone pushed through the crowd. To George's relief it was the bouncer who had been checking ID's and collecting the cover charge at the door. He was at least as large as

Sean. "You're gone, buddy," the bouncer said. "Owner's request."

Sean wheeled toward him. "Who are *you?*" he demanded.

The bouncer smiled. "You really want to find out?"

George couldn't believe it, but Sean actually took a step toward the bouncer. Sean deserved anything he got for his behavior, but George didn't want to witness a bloody battle.

"Hey, Sean," she blurted out. "Getting picked up for assault won't have the best effect on your football scholarship."

George's words seemed to stop the big athlete. He paused and scowled at the bouncer, and then at George. Finally he turned and plowed his way through the crowd.

Shaking her head, George watched him go. "Mara went out with *that* thing?" Will said in disbelief.

"Apparently," George remarked. "Although it seems hard to believe. I just wonder if he's ever going to accept that it's over."

Suddenly Jake appeared in the crowd and pushed his way toward them. "Are you okay? For a while there it looked like you were about to become the *Times*'s next headline."

"We're fine. Thanks, Jake," George said, glancing toward Will. He was glaring at the door, which was just closing behind Sean.

He was obviously still seething. "Don't even

think of doing anything about this," she warned him.

"Yeah, Will," Jake chimed in. "That guy looks pretty rough."

Will nodded, but he didn't say anything.

As George turned back toward Jake, she noticed a woman standing beside him. She had raven black hair and eyes the color of deep brown mahogany. Her fair white skin made her dark features seem all the more exotic and intriguing. George thought she was the same girl she'd seen Jake with the day before when they were walking outside the coffee shop.

Noticing George's gaze, Jake brought the woman forward. "George, Nadia. Nadia, George. And her boyfriend, Will Blackfeather."

Nadia—George thought. For some reason the name rang a bell.

"It's a pleasure to meet you," Nadia said amiably, offering her hand.

As George took her hand, she recognized the girl's accent as Russian. It also explained why her name was familiar, George realized with a pang.

Oh, no, she thought, still smiling at Nadia. What is Nancy going to say when she finds out that her new suitemate is also Jake's new girlfriend?

Nancy took a thick wool sweater from her closet and pulled it on over her black turtleneck and black jeans. In a few minutes she was meeting Bess downstairs to go to a late-night screening of *The Maltese Falcon*. Neither of them had a date—or wanted one, for that matter. Nancy was looking forward to spending time with Bess and seeing the old movie.

Just as she was about to grab her coat and head out the door, her phone rang.

"Nancy? I'm glad I caught you."

"Bess?" Nancy asked. "Aren't you supposed to be downstairs right now?"

"Well," Bess said. "I know I said I'd like to go to this movie, but I just can't do it now."

"Why not? What's wrong?"

"I just can't go to a place where I'll be surrounded by Twizzlers and Milk Duds and popcorn," Bess replied with a moan.

"Are you joking?" Nancy laughed. "Don't be so silly, Bess. We just won't get anything."

"It might sound dumb, but I don't trust myself right now," Bess said. "I'd rather not go at all."

"Well, okay," Nancy said slowly. "I don't really care about the movie. I'd like to see you, though. Let's do something else instead."

"Ummm, I don't think so," Bess said softly. "I'm sorry, Nancy, but I'm really tired. All I want to do right now is go to sleep."

"Are you okay, Bess?" Nancy asked, worried. First, Bess had sounded so obsessed with food. And now she was complaining about being tired.

"I'm fine, really," Bess assured Nancy. She gave a feeble laugh. "You know me, I'm always cranky when I start a new diet. But if I get a good night's sleep, I'll feel much better tomorrow."

"Okay, but listen, if you need me I'll be here," Nancy said. "Even if you just want to get together and hang out. So give me a call if you change your mind."

"Thanks, Nancy," Bess said, the relief sounding in her voice. "I will."

With a sigh, Nancy put the phone down and pulled off her sweater. So much for her exciting Saturday night plans. Nancy knew she could go to the film by herself if she wanted—but it didn't seem as much fun without Bess. Besides, she had promised Bess she'd be in if she needed her.

She could use a quiet night to herself, Nancy decided. Tomorrow morning she had another early photo shoot with Gary.

Nancy was about to pull out her books and start working on her English paper when the phone rang again.

Nancy picked it up with a smile. Leave it to Bess to change her mind about going out in less than two seconds.

"So you're coming?" she said into the receiver.

"Excuse me?" a woman's voice asked. "Is this Nancy? Nancy, it's Avery."

Nancy felt as if she'd been punched in the stomach. "Avery?" she managed to choke out as she sank down onto her bed. Avery Fallon was just about the last person in the world she wanted to talk to right then, or probably ever.

"Listen, Nancy," Avery began. "I had to call you. I hope you won't be angry, but Hannah told me about the surprise party you were planning."

"She did?" Nancy echoed, feeling betrayed.

"Yes, and I'm just so sorry I didn't think to tell you about the weekend plans I'd made," Avery said in a rush. "It's just that your father's been working so hard, and I thought a vacation—even for a day or two—would help him to relax. After Hannah told me about what you've been planning, I decided to call you. I can certainly change our plans so your party can still happen," Avery went on. "In fact, I think it would be wonderful for your dad. I know he'd really appreciate it."

Nancy's fingers tightened on the phone. *I think it would be wonderful . . . I know he'd really appreciate it.*

Does Avery really think she needs to tell me what *my* father would appreciate?

"Nancy?" Avery said. "What do you think about that? Do you want to go ahead with the party?"

"Oh, no," Nancy said coldly. She was furious and filled with a deadly calm. "I wouldn't want to spoil *your* perfect weekend with *my* party."

"I just tried to explain, Nancy," Avery began. "I'm trying to involve you in—"

"Oh, don't worry about me," Nancy cut in. "I'll just drop a birthday card in the mail for Dad. He'll probably appreciate that as much as a party with all his friends."

"Come on, Nancy." Avery sounded angry herself, but Nancy wasn't interested in hearing anything more from her father's girlfriend.

"Thanks again for calling," she said. "I hope you two have a wonderful time celebrating Dad's birthday." With that, Nancy slammed down the phone.

CHAPTER 8

Casey opened one eye, then the other. As she raised her head off the pillow, she remembered it was Sunday morning, then dropped it back down.

"I *love* Sunday mornings," she murmured, letting her eyes close again.

"Me, too," Nadia replied from across the room.

Casey's eyes flew wide open. She had gotten so used to sharing a room with her old roommate, Stephanie, that the Russian accent had taken her completely by surprise.

She sat up and peered at Nadia. "I totally forgot I had a new roommate," she said with a smile.

Nadia propped herself up on one elbow in bed and smiled. "I hope I don't bother you," she said sweetly.

"After living with Stephanie, no one can

bother me," Casey joked. She started combing out her hair with her fingers. Then she looked across at Nadia and sighed. "How can you look so good so early?" she complained.

Nadia was as radiant first thing in the morning as she was at night. She was, as Stephanie might have said, drop-dead gorgeous. But the most attractive thing about Nadia, Casey thought, was that Nadia didn't seem to know how good-looking she was. Casey had only known her for two days, but she already liked Nadia.

"Actually," Nadia said, "that is what your suitemates told me about you. How you can look so good in the morning with so little effort. They said I should not get too upset by it."

Casey laughed. "I hope you're comfortable in the room," she said. "Are you sleeping well?"

A shock of black hair fell in front of Nadia's face, and she drew it behind her ear. "Actually, I haven't even been to sleep yet. I've been lying awake all night."

Concerned, Casey sat up, tugging at her Wilder U. nightshirt. "Is everything okay?"

Nadia wrinkled her nose. "Better than okay."

"Oh!" Casey grinned as what Nadia was saying sank in. "You met a guy. And in how many hours? Less than forty-eight?"

Nadia laughed. "So, I met him two days ago."

Casey slipped out of her bed, and went over to sit on the edge of Nadia's bed. "Okay, maybe nobody's told you yet, but there's an old American college tradition—you have to tell your roommate everything. So let's go—spill the beans. Who is it?"

Suddenly Nadia's smile fell. She shook her head. "I didn't know," she murmured.

"What are you talking about, Nadia?" Casey said, confused.

"You know him," Nadia said, looking straight into Casey's eyes.

"I do?" Casey squinted, scrolling through her mental lists of men. Who on earth had Nadia fallen for already? "Okay, I'm assuming he's gorgeous. I mean, he has to be, right?"

Nadia nodded shyly.

"Well, if I had Stephanie's little black book I'd have the name of every available—and not-so-available—gorgeous guy on campus. Because believe me, honey"—she threw a theatrical wink—"Stephanie's been through them all."

But Nadia shook her head. "Not this one."

Casey furrowed her brow. "You know, Nadia, if I didn't know that my boyfriend was in Los Angeles right now, I'd be worried."

Outside in the hallway came the sounds of a closing door. After all this time at Wilder, Casey could tell who was doing what in suite

301 just by the sounds. Everyone had her own way of walking. Every door had its own way of closing.

"Hi, Nancy!" Casey called out.

"Hey, Case," Nancy's hushed voice filtered through the closed door. "Gotta run. I have to meet Gary for a photo shoot and I'm already late."

" 'Bye," Casey called.

When Casey looked back at Nadia, her roommate had a stricken look on her face. Casey tilted her head, trying to read the anxiety in Nadia's eyes.

Then it struck her.

"No," she said softly. "You and *Jake Collins?*"

Nadia nodded silently.

"Uh-oh . . ." Casey murmured.

"What will Nancy say when she finds out?" Nadia asked in a worried tone.

"I don't know," Casey admitted. "Boy," she added, "between Stephanie's marriage and your going out with Jake, this suite is getting to be like *Melrose Place!*"

"Melrose Place," Nadia repeated. "Excuse me, but what is that?"

Casey grinned. "It's kind of like a soap opera, Nadia."

As Nancy trudged across the deserted campus to the *Wilder Times* office, she found herself replaying her disastrous phone conversation with Avery in her mind.

Good thing I'm seeing Gary this morning, she thought. He'd been helpful before—maybe she could talk to him again. The truth was, she was feeling embarrassed by the way she'd spoken to Avery. She'd acted so childish, and she wished she hadn't hung up like that.

Still, Avery had no right planning Dad's birthday without consulting me, she thought. She just barges in and—yes—ruins everything!

By the time Nancy got to the *Wilder Times* office, she was fuming again. She looked around for Gary, expecting to find him asleep in the pillow-pit or somewhere.

"Wake up, sleeping beauty," she called out. But the pit and the couch in the lounge area were empty. There was no sign of Gary or his photo equipment.

"Hmm . . ." she said, reaching for the phone. She dialed Gary's room at Plimpton Hall, but there was no answer. His answering machine didn't even pick up.

"That's weird," Nancy said, checking her watch. It was a quarter after eight. Gary was late.

He must be on his way, she decided. Maybe he stopped for a bagel and coffee, or . . .

A grin slowly spread across Nancy's face. Hadn't George said that Mara and Gary might go out again last night? Maybe the night had been so much fun that night had turned into morning.

Nancy waited a while longer, then decided to leave. She was a little disappointed that she wouldn't get to tell Gary about Avery's call, but mostly she felt happy for him. Obviously, he and Mara were hitting it off.

Quickly Nancy called down to the boathouse to tell the coach of the crew team that the shoot would have to be rescheduled. They set up another date, then Nancy left the building. As she started across the quad, she decided to have breakfast at Java Joe's. Maybe she'd bump into some friends there.

As Nancy headed for the coffee shop, an ambulance went screaming past, its emergency lights flashing. She whipped her head around, following its path into the Plimpton Hall parking lot. A moment later two campus police cars and a Weston town police car roared up the street and followed the ambulance to Plimpton.

What's up? Nancy wondered. Instinctively, she turned around and started sprinting toward the commotion.

A crowd had gathered on the walk near where the ambulance and the police cars had pulled up. Nancy saw paramedics running back and forth, unloading equipment from the ambulance and running with it to the center of the crowd. Someone, she could see, was stretched out on the asphalt.

Plimpton Hall was five stories high. Most of the windows facing the parking lot were open, and students were leaning out to see what was going on. Several of them were distraught, Nancy noticed. Two girls on the second floor were holding each other around the shoulders, and a guy wearing a soccer jersey had a hand cupped over his mouth. On the ground several students were sobbing.

Nancy's heart skipped a beat. Obviously something terrible had happened. She didn't want to imagine the worst. She stopped at the edge of the crowd. "What's going on?" she asked as she edged her way toward the center.

"Somebody fell," a guy mumbled.

"Or jumped," somebody else chimed in.

Nancy's body registered her shock before her brain did. First, her knees went loose, and then her hands went numb. Finally she heard her own voice shrieking.

"Gary? Oh my gosh—it's Gary!"

Nancy's friend lay sprawled on the sidewalk, his legs and arms splayed at funny angles. The paramedics were a blur of activity as they frantically tried to revive him. Nancy looked up at the dorm again, and this time she noticed an officer sticking his head out of a third-floor window.

"I can't believe he jumped," the girl next to

Nancy whispered. "He didn't seem depressed or anything."

Jumped? Nancy leaned over the paramedics to get a look. Gary's face was ashen and his eyes were shut tight.

Suddenly one of the paramedics stood up. "Time," he said hopelessly, waving at the three other people still surrounding Gary. The two men who'd been performing CPR slowly gave up, and a woman who'd been ready with portable electric shock mitts put them back into their case and snapped it shut.

A murmur went through the crowd.

"He was gone before we got here," the first paramedic said. "Looks like a suicide."

Gone? Jumped? Suicide?

The paramedic unfolded a white plastic sheet and let it float down over Gary's body.

"Oh no," Nancy gasped in horror. She covered her eyes, hoping to erase the image. But when she lowered her hands, the facts were right in front of her: the still shape of Gary's body under the white sheet.

Nancy choked back her sobs as several people in the crowd began wailing and crying. "It's time for everyone to get back to their rooms," one of the local police officers said firmly. "There's nothing anyone can do. It's all over, folks."

Nancy was wiping away tears as another car pulled up at the edge of the crowd. Nancy recognized the man who stepped out as the dean of undergraduate studies. He hurried over to the police and then began helping the cops herd everyone away from the scene. Nancy stepped aside as the paramedics carried Gary's body into the ambulance.

Her whole body was numb. Why would Gary have committed suicide? she thought. Everything in his life was going so well. He'd just won a big photography prize and had two dates with Mara. . . .

Abruptly Nancy remembered the jokes Gary had made the day before after his run-in with Sean Masters. He'd said he valued his life and she'd better get all the photos she could out of him while she had the chance.

At the time they'd seemed like stupid jokes between friends. But now . . .

Fresh tears began streaming down Nancy's cheeks. She couldn't believe this had really happened.

The campus police continued to usher students back to their rooms. Somehow she wasn't ready to move away from Gary's dorm yet.

As her eyes scanned the scene, she noticed a tall, slim guy wearing a Toledo Mudhens baseball cap standing with his back against the brick wall of Plimpton Hall, a miserable expression in his face. Wait a minute, Nancy thought. Hadn't Gary told her his roommate always wore a Toledo Mudhens cap?

Nancy stood and hurried over to the tall guy. "Are you Trevor?" she asked.

His backpack was slung over his shoulder and his hands were rooted deep in his pockets. He stared without focusing at the spot where Gary had lain, just shaking his head. "I can't believe it," he said over and over. "I can't believe it."

"Hey," Nancy said, putting her hand on his shoulder. "Are you Trevor?"

"What? Yeah, I'm Trevor," the guy said, blinking at her.

"I'm Nancy, Gary's friend. He was supposed to meet me this morning—"

"Yeah, he said something about it last night." Trevor nodded.

"Were you home when Gary . . ." Nancy's words trailed off. She couldn't bring herself to say "jumped." She just refused to believe it. "Were you home when this happened?" she finished.

Trevor just shook his head and stammered, "I-I've been at the chem lab. Since six. Gary was sleeping like a rock when I left. I can't believe this happened."

Nancy took Trevor's hand and gave it a squeeze. It felt cold and limp. As she looked at him, she saw that Trevor's eyes were pale blue and his face was pale, as if he spent all his time indoors. This was the roommate who drove Gary nuts by studying all the time and humming along to his Walkman. That seemed so petty and beside the point now.

"Trevor," Nancy said softly, struggling to hold back her own tears. "You don't think Gary would have jumped, do you?"

"But that's what they're saying," he said, confused.

"But what do *you* think? You lived with him. I mean, was he upset or mad about anything yesterday?"

A trace of a smile crossed Trevor's face. "Only that I studied so much and I wouldn't let him sleep. But otherwise he was psyched about everything. He was psyched about life."

Nancy nodded. "Right. Exactly. Gary was happy. He wasn't depressed. I just can't picture him committing suicide," she went on. "It doesn't fit with his personality."

Trevor shifted his backpack. "I'm due back at the lab," he said. Nancy nodded silently and watched Trevor walk slowly away.

Nancy turned as the police cars and ambulance pulled away from the curb. The ambulance lights were off, and the siren was silent. This time there was no reason for it to hurry anywhere. She felt a cold shiver travel up her spine. Gary's dead. The realization hit her hard.

The last group of students were heading

back into the building. As she watched them go, Nancy noticed something lying in the grass near where they had stood. She walked over to get a better look.

Her heart started beating fast. That's Gary's favorite camera, she realized. It was a Leica, an old and expensive brand, and Gary had bragged about it like a father bragging about his perfect son. But now the lens was smashed and the back of the camera was broken off its hinges. Had it fallen with him? she wondered. And why hadn't the police picked it up?

Nancy knelt and lifted the broken camera into her lap. There was a canister of film still in it, but it wasn't threaded. In fact, it looked like a finished roll that had just been rewound. Nancy pulled the lever and the roll of film popped out.

"Why would he jump with his camera?" she thought out loud, staring at the film in the palm of her hand. "That's so weird. None of this makes any sense."

Nancy stuck the film and camera in her backpack so that she could take it to the police. She stood and looked up at Gary's window.

"I have no idea what happened," she said under her breath. "But one thing's for sure. Gary didn't commit suicide. It had to have been an accident, or . . ."

Her eyes drifted down from the window. "Or murder," she whispered hoarsely.

Bam! Bam!

"George?" Pam Miller's groggy voice called across the room. "George? Is the building falling down?"

Slowly George blinked her eyes open.

BAM! BAM! BAM!

Instantly, the banging seemed to grow louder.

"No, but the door's about to cave in," she muttered back to Pam.

George pulled herself out of bed and grabbed her robe. Then she checked her bedside clock—it was 9:00 A.M.

"Doesn't the world know it's Sunday?" Pam moaned, her head under two pillows. "People get to sleep in on Sundays."

"George, are you in there?" a frantic voice came from the hall.

George opened the door, and immediately she was wide-awake. Nancy was standing outside in the hallway—her face as white as a sheet.

"What's wrong?" George blurted out. Then a thought occurred to her. "Did you hear the news?"

"I didn't just hear," Nancy said numbly. "I saw it myself."

"You saw Nadia and Jake?" George said.

"What?" Nancy asked.

George drew back. From the confused expression on Nancy's face, George could tell that Nancy had no idea what George was referring to. But Nancy was definitely upset about something else.

"Forget it," George said quickly. "What's the matter? What are you talking about?"

"It's Gary," Nancy said, her voice catching. Tears streamed down her face. "I can't really believe it, but he's dead."

George was stunned.

Across the room, Pam had come awake, too. As Nancy stepped into the room, Pam sat up in bed.

"What?" George managed finally. "Are you serious?" But George could tell that Nancy was only too serious.

Nancy hadn't even heard George's question. "He jumped out a window," she murmured. "Or at least, that's how it looks."

Suddenly George felt sick. Her mind raced back to the last time she had seen Gary and everything Mara had told her about their date.

Mara! George drew in a deep breath. "Does Mara know?" she asked Nancy.

"No, I don't think so. That's why I came over here. Do you think you could tell her? It might be easier for her to hear it from a friend. If it can be easier," Nancy added.

"How awful," said Pam. "Poor Gary."

"I know." Nancy shook her head. "It makes no sense," she said. She grabbed a handful of tissues as she turned to go. "So you'll talk to Mara?"

"Yeah, I'll talk to her," replied George heavily. But how was she going to tell Mara the terrible news that Gary was dead?

"Hello?" Nancy called as she knocked on the open door to Gary and Trevor's room at Plimpton Hall.

Nancy had to come. Nancy didn't want to bother Trevor, but she had to see what else she could find out. She knew she wouldn't be able to concentrate on anything until she found out how Gary had died.

A man in an overcoat filled the doorway. "Sorry, miss. Police investigation. You'll have to move away from the door now."

"I was Gary's friend," Nancy said. "I . . ." Her voice trailed off as she looked past the man into the room. It was so weird to see all of Gary's things, when he himself . . .

The officer softened when he saw the grief on her face. "I'm sorry. It's difficult to lose a friend this way."

"There's no way Gary would have committed suicide," Nancy blurted out.

The man shrugged. "You know, I've been doing this job for a long time. A lot of the things I've learned on the job have surprised me. And one thing that's surprised me the most is that friends and family are usually the last people to know how truly depressed someone is."

"This case is different," Nancy protested. "Gary had too many good things going on in his life to want it to end. He wanted to be a professional photographer. And he was falling in love—"

The officer held up a hand to signal their conversation had come to an end. "I believe you, miss. Look, I shouldn't even be talking to you. Let me just finish up in here."

"Was there a suicide note?" Nancy called after him as he walked away.

"That's confidential information right now," he called back. "Look, I'm sorry. This must be difficult. But I have work to do. Please don't cross into the room, okay?"

The officer wandered over to Gary's dresser and picked at his things, lifting up photographs, peering at them, and putting them down to take notes. Nancy knew she should go, but she couldn't help herself. As she glanced at Gary's desk, she spotted a note pinned to the shelf above it. While the officer had his back turned, she leaned in the room to get a better look.

My life isn't worth living anymore.
That's why I've decided to end it.
Sayonara. G.

What? Everything inside Nancy rebelled as she read the note. It sounds nothing like Gary, she thought. He was thrilled about lots of things and had a ton of friends. And just yesterday he'd joked that he wasn't ready to lose his life after Sean Masters had threatened him. Why would he suddenly sound so despairing? And "Sayonara"?

"There's no way Gary wrote that," Nancy said out loud.

The officer whirled around. "Hey, I told you not to come in here," he said, irritated. He strode over to the door. "I'm going to have to close this now."

"I didn't go inside," Nancy insisted. "Listen to me. That's not Gary's note. He couldn't have written it. And what it says isn't true. He loved photography, and he'd just won a big prize. Besides that, he'd just started going out with this girl he's had a crush on for a while."

The officer's face turned bright red. "Maybe you're right, young lady. But this is our business, not yours. If you have any real evidence, then I'd love to hear it." The officer stared down at her, waiting. "I'm all ears."

Nancy opened her mouth, about to blurt out what had happened with Sean Masters. But the truth was that Nancy didn't have any evidence— at least not yet. And she didn't want to make any accusations without proof. She was going to have to poke around on her own before she talked to the police about her suspicions.

Reluctantly she shook her head. "Never mind," she mumbled. Then she took off down the hall.

Nancy didn't know exactly what she was looking for, but she knew exactly where she was going to start looking—by asking Mara some questions about Sean Masters.

CHAPTER 9

Come in!" Mara called through the door.

George took a deep breath and twisted the knob on Mara's door. She'd prepared a speech in her head while walking from her dorm to Mara's, but now that she was about to see Mara, the words vanished. There was nothing good to say and no good way to say it.

Taking a deep breath, George went in. "Hey," she said as cheerily as she could.

"Hello, George," Mara said, smiling. Obviously she hadn't heard about Gary yet. "Are you making the Sunday visiting rounds?" she joked.

"Uh, not exactly," George replied. She noticed that Mara had a book propped up in front of her and two piles of index cards flanking her on either side. "Are you working on a term paper?" she asked.

Mara sighed. "A monster. The legacy of

World War Two in France. Unfortunately, I'm a little distracted these days. The paper was going great until Friday night."

George lowered herself onto Mara's bed. "What was Friday night?" she asked, afraid to hear the answer.

"My first date with Gary," Mara announced happily. "You know, the one where I realized that dating could be a truly pleasant experience with the right person?"

The grin on Mara's face was so wide and sincere that George could almost feel her own heart breaking.

She slid closer to Mara's desk. "Mara, I have something to tell you."

Mara shut the book that was open in front of her. "Good. I'm open to any form of procrastination," she joked. "Did you bring any food with you? Chocolate? Want to go see a movie?"

"Mara," George said soberly, "what I have to tell you is not good."

Mara's eyes suddenly narrowed and her lips pursed. "Is anything wrong?"

George nodded. "I have some terrible news. It's about Gary."

Mara looked confused. "Gary? What happened?" she asked nervously.

George couldn't reply.

Mara's eyes began to moisten. "George, what happened? What are you telling me?"

George blinked away her own tears. She clutched Mara's hands. "Mara, Gary's—I don't know how to say this—but Gary's dead."

"What?" Mara cried. She looked at George as if her friend had grown two heads. "What are you talking about, Gary's dead?" Her face drained of color as George nodded. "Oh my gosh. You're serious, aren't you? But how? Why?"

In a shaky voice, George told Mara everything Nancy had told her about Gary being found on the ground outside Plimpton Hall.

Mara stared at her hands. "I can't believe it. I mean, I know you're sitting here telling me this, but I swear I don't believe it. Gary's so— alive, such a sweet person. I don't understand."

George lay a consoling hand on her shoulder. "You're in shock, Mara. It's okay. It's going to take time to process this." George cleared her throat. "You don't think that Gary actually would have—" She couldn't even finish the sentence.

But Mara could. "Jump? Commit suicide?" she said. She shook her head. "I never would have thought so. Never in a million years." Abruptly, Mara collapsed against George. "This is a nightmare," she moaned. "Just when I thought—" A loud sob choked off her words.

George held Mara, gently rocking her back

and forth as Mara cried. She knew there was nothing else she could do.

It's going to take time, she told herself, remembering how Bess was still having trouble dealing with Paul Cody's death. It's just going to take time.

As the elevator doors opened, Nancy could see a couple of girls loitering outside Mara's room. By now, news of Gary's death had spread all over campus. Mara, as the woman he liked, was obviously going to be the object of everyone's sympathy, and curiosity, she thought ruefully.

"How is she?" Nancy asked one of the girls.

One of them shrugged. "How would you be?" she murmured.

"Not good," Nancy admitted. As she leaned closer to the door, she could hear George's hushed voice. Nancy pushed open the door and found Mara and George sitting on the bed. Mara's face was tear streaked and red.

"Mara, I'm so sorry," Nancy said instantly.

Mara nodded and gave her a weak smile. "Me, too, Nancy, for you. I mean, I liked Gary a lot, but you two were closer than we were. You've known him a lot longer."

"I don't know if Gary told you," Nancy said, "but he'd had a crush on you since the first day of freshman orientation."

Fresh tears welled up in Mara's eyes. "He

didn't tell me that," she said in a pained whisper.

Sighing, Nancy sat on the bed with them. "For what it's worth, I just want you guys to know that I'm positive Gary did not commit suicide."

"We are, too," George replied. "It doesn't make sense."

"A lot of things aren't making sense," Nancy said. "First of all, his camera was lying on the ground next to him." She told the girls about how she'd found his old Leica.

"Why would he jump with his camera?" George asked.

"He wouldn't," Nancy told her. "And then I saw this weird suicide note in his room. It sounded nothing like him." Nancy shook her head. "It even said 'Sayonara' on the bottom. It was more like a bad joke than a suicide note."

Mara raised her tear-streaked face. "But if Gary didn't write it, then who did?"

"I don't know," Nancy said. "Mara, if it's not too painful to talk about this, I want to ask you something."

Mara shrugged. "Try me."

"What was Gary like last night when you guys went out? Did he seem different? Like he had anything on his mind?"

Mara didn't say anything.

"Did you go to a movie or something?" Nancy prodded her gently.

"Uh—a movie," Mara said, shifting her eyes toward the window.

Nancy tilted her head, puzzled by the change in Mara's attitude.

"What movie did you see?" she asked.

But Mara just stared stonily out the window, as if she were in a trance. Then George shrugged, obviously as confused as Nancy was.

"Actually," Mara began, "I don't know what I'm saying." She shook her head. "It must be the shock, I guess. I actually didn't see Gary last night."

"What?" Nancy said. "You just said you saw him and that you went to a movie!"

"I know," Mara replied. "I'm sorry. I'm just a little dazed." She took a deep breath.

"I was here last night," she went on. "Alone. I didn't talk to Gary, or anyone."

"But didn't you two have a date?" Nancy was more confused than ever. "Gary told me you were getting together again."

"I canceled on him," Mara said sharply. Then she stood up as if she didn't want to talk about it, or anything, anymore.

"Oh," Nancy said, troubled. She couldn't read Mara, couldn't make sense of her behavior at all.

Finally Nancy stood and zipped up her jacket. "I think I'm going to head out for a while and get some fresh air. I'm not feeling that great. You're okay?" she mouthed to George.

George nodded. "I'll stay here a bit longer."

Crossing the campus back to Thayer, Nancy was lost in her thoughts. She noticed almost nothing going on around her—the small knots of students gathered outside the Student Union, on the steps of the administration building, outside Hewlitt Performing Arts Center, all talking about Gary's death.

I know Mara was upset by the news, but how could she make a mistake about what she did just the night before? Nancy wondered. She didn't seem sure whether she'd seen Gary or not. Now *that's* weird.

Nancy wished she'd had the chance to question Mara about the threats that Sean Masters had made to Gary. But Mara was so spaced out by the news about Gary that Nancy hadn't wanted to upset her further.

I've got to track Sean down as soon as possible, she thought. If anyone had a motive for harming Gary, it was Sean.

"Nancy!"

Nancy looked up. She was so deep in thought that it took her a minute to recognize where she was. She'd made it into her suite, and there was Nadia in a sexy gauzy robe outside her door.

"I'm so sorry about your friend," Nadia went on.

"Thanks, Nadia," Nancy replied. "It is a terrible tragedy."

Nancy opened the door to her room and collapsed on her bed. Nadia followed her in and sat on the edge of Kara's.

Nadia was clasping and unclasping her hands, as if she had something on her mind. "I knew someone who did that," she said sadly. "Suicide is so difficult to understand."

Nancy shook her head forcefully. "Gary didn't jump," she insisted. "He would never do it."

"Oh," Nadia replied, confused. "Then his death is both tragic *and* alarming. If he did not kill himself, then . . ." Her words hung in the air for a second.

"I don't mean to be rude, but this is upsetting me," Nancy said, rubbing her head. She was exhausted.

"You're right," Nadia replied. "I'm sorry." She stood up and took a step toward the door.

"No, don't go," Nancy said apologetically. "I'm glad for the company. It's just that I'd rather talk about something else, something happy. Like, are you enjoying Wilder?"

Nadia gave her a big nod. "Oh, yes. I couldn't be more happy."

"So what did you do last night?" Nancy asked. "Were you at Club Z?"

Nancy was surprised to see Nadia's face turn deep red. Nancy chuckled. "Wow, it must have been something *really* good."

"I had a date," Nadia mumbled.

"Well, you sure didn't waste time . . ." Nancy started to say as something clicked inside her brain. Hadn't George said something about Nadia and Jake?

Nancy looked at her new suitemate with sudden interest. "Nadia, who were you out with?" she asked slowly.

A pained expression filled Nadia's eyes. "I don't know how to tell you this . . ." she mumbled. "But a very dashing guy interviewed me about transferring here, and we went out, and I had *no* idea who he was. I like you so much, Nancy, and I'd do anything not to hurt you, and if it upsets you, I'll never see him again."

"Whoa!" Nancy held up her hand for Nadia to stop. "First of all, are you telling me that you went on a date last night with Jake Collins?"

Nadia nodded, embarrassed.

Nancy exhaled, trying to take measure of her own feelings. How did she feel—sad? Angry? Jealous? Confused? She wasn't really sure.

Since she and Jake had broken up, Nancy had been very distracted, both by meeting Judd and by her thoughts about Ned Nickerson. Nancy had even thought that she and Ned might actually get together again. But Nancy hadn't really given much thought to her feelings about Jake since their breakup.

"That's it," Nadia declared, reaching for Nancy's phone. "I can see you're upset. I'm calling him right away."

Calmly, Nancy put her hand on Nadia's, stopping her. "Actually," she said, "it's fine."

"It is?" Nadia asked in a small voice.

Nancy nodded. "Jake's wonderful. It might be a little awkward at times," she admitted. "But I'll deal with it."

"Really?" Happily, Nadia chattered on about what a great time she'd had with Jake the night before, dinner, dancing at Club Z, a long walk . . .

As Nancy listened, the smile never left her face. But inside, a part of her felt sad and very much alone.

You're just being overly emotional because of Gary's death, she told herself. Still, she had the sudden feeling that seeing Jake with Nadia would be harder than she'd let on.

"I know this is probably hard to believe right now," Bess said softly, "but you'll get through this, Mara."

It was Sunday evening, and Bess was with George and Nancy in Mara Lindon's dorm room. A short while after George had delivered the tragic news about Gary's death to

Mara, she'd called Bess to ask her if she'd come and talk to Mara.

Boy, I can't believe I've become such an expert on grief, Bess thought as she listened to herself speak.

There were still times when she thought of Paul and felt like giving up, but she had made it through so far. Maybe her presence would give Mara some support.

"The hardest part will be acting normal and doing normal things," Mara choked out. "I mean, doing things like going to class will seem so disrespectful."

"I know. It's hard to understand why the whole world doesn't stop when something like this happens," Bess agreed.

Mara looked up at Bess.

"One of the most important things you need to do, Mara, is allow yourself time to grieve. It's okay if you don't want to go to class tomorrow—if you need time to put this in perspective."

"Maybe you could talk to someone," George suggested. "The counselors on campus are really good. Right, Bess?"

"Definitely," Bess agreed. "Talking can be helpful." She flushed as she remembered she had blown off an appointment with her own counselor recently. She knew it was important for her to continue talking about her feelings— even when she was totally sick of hearing herself. "Listen, Mara," she continued. "If you want to go to class tomorrow—maybe to have something to focus on—don't feel guilty about that. It won't mean that you're being disrespectful to Gary."

Instantly, Mara's face turned red, and a tear started rolling down her cheek. "I was thinking about my anthropology class. There's a presentation I'm supposed to give. It's such a little thing. No big deal. But I really worked hard on it, and all I keep thinking is that I want to go." Stricken, she looked at Bess. "Isn't that awful?"

"No!" Bess cried. "That's exactly the point. Gary is dead. It's awful and horrible and none of us understands why. And we all have to learn to accept it. But finding ways to feel good about ourselves and keeping life normal is the only thing that can help us find perspective. Life does go on, Mara. No one is going to blame you for continuing to live."

"Are you sure?" Mara asked. She shook her head and wiped the tears from her eyes. "It's true I didn't know Gary that well," she admitted, "but I really liked him. I mean, I thought he was a special person."

"He was," Nancy agreed. "A wonderful person."

Instantly Mara's tears were back.

Watching her, Bess remembered the wells of despair she'd felt after Paul's death. Before she even realized it, she was rocking back and forth, just like Mara, trying to calm herself and keep her own pain in check.

Somewhere in her mind, she realized that she was eating. George had brought over food for Mara—snacks and sweets—anything to cheer her up and feed her in case she didn't feel up to going to the dining hall for dinner. But it wasn't Mara who needed the food. It was Bess. And she sat and ate and listened to Mara and tried to keep all the painful feelings from coming back.

George pushed slowly through the doors of Mara's dorm and out into the chilly night. But it was more than the weather that made her shiver, and she hugged herself tightly. She turned to Bess and Nancy, who were right behind her.

"You think she'll be okay?" George asked.

"She'll be up and down," Bess said. "She'll be able to laugh as if nothing happened one minute, then the next, when she feels like picking up the phone to call Gary, she'll fall to pieces."

George and Nancy exchanged glances behind Bess. Losing Paul to an accident had changed Bess forever. She had experienced a lot of pain, but she'd also become a lot wiser.

"Maybe you can give Mara a call in the next

few days," Nancy suggested. "You might be her most valuable friend right now."

"Sure," Bess replied.

They walked a minute in silence. A sheet made into a sign hung from the arches above the Student Union. The word *S-U-I-C-I-D-E* was written on the sheet with a big red *X* through it. Talk to a Counselor, read the sign. Talk to a Friend. Just Talk to Someone!

"I'm glad they put that up," Nancy said. "A lot of kids will be thinking about Gary as if he did commit suicide. I want everyone to know there are other options when you're depressed."

George nodded. "There are lots of places to go for help," she agreed.

"Actually, I've been wanting to run something by you guys," Nancy went on.

"Me, too," George said, relieved. Something had been hounding her ever since she'd first heard the news. She quickly told them about the incident with Sean Masters at Club Z, and how he was prepared to do major structural damage to anybody who so much as looked at Mara the wrong way.

"You're right on my wavelength, George. Sean Masters is the person I wanted to talk about, too," Nancy said.

Bess shook her head, confused. "What are you guys talking about? You think Gary was murdered? Don't you think that's a little dramatic?"

"It wasn't suicide, Bess," George said.

"Well, maybe he just fell. Accidents happen, you know," Bess said.

"But there was a note," Nancy reminded her. She looked at George. "Did you tell Mara about the scene at Club Z?" Nancy asked her.

George shook her head. "It didn't seem to be the right time to bring it up."

Nancy nodded. "First thing tomorrow, I'm going to look up Sean's address in the student directory."

Bess was still doubtful. "Before you hunt down Sean, maybe you should talk to Gary's roommate. He could know something about Gary that we don't."

"I've talked to Trevor," Nancy said with a sigh. "But he wasn't very helpful. Still, I'll pay him a visit tomorrow, too."

CHAPTER 10

"Trevor, are you there? Trevor?"

It was late Monday morning, and Nancy had been knocking for at least a minute on Trevor and Gary's door. She'd found out that Sean Masters lived off campus, and she planned to visit him later. Right now she was taking Bess's suggestion and visiting Trevor again.

As Nancy knocked again, the bathroom door across the hall opened and a guy in a robe came out, toweling his hair.

"Do you know if Trevor is here?" Nancy asked.

"He went in there after the police left on Sunday and he hasn't come out since," the guy replied.

"Go away!" Trevor called from inside.

Nancy pursed her lips and tried the knob. It was locked. "Trevor, I know you're upset," Nancy called through the crack. "But I'm

Gary's friend. I was the one who talked to you yesterday."

Suddenly the lock clicked and the door swung open. Trevor was standing there, disheveled in sweatpants and a ratty T-shirt. The blinds on the window had been drawn shut and the room was completely dark.

"Are you okay?" Nancy asked.

"How would you be?" he replied bitterly. "People have been calling me and knocking at my door all morning."

Nancy followed him in and shut the door behind her. She noticed the phone was unplugged from the phone jack, but otherwise the room looked just as it had the day before, minus the suicide note. Gary's bed was made, and his book bag hung from the back of his chair, as if it were ready to be ferried to class.

A wave of sadness washed over Nancy. Tonight would probably be the first time Nancy would go to the *Wilder Times* office and not see Gary. She could still picture him asleep against the fence at the tennis courts. And she remembered the way he'd listened to her talk about her dad and Avery. She was really going to miss his friendship and all the funny comments he made at the newspaper staff meetings.

"Are you going to the memorial service at the *Times*'s office tonight?" Trevor asked her suddenly.

"Yes," Nancy replied. "Are you?"

Trevor shook his head. "I don't think so," he muttered. Then he waved a hand toward Gary's side of the room. "Take whatever you want. It's weird just to have his stuff around."

"I think maybe I'll leave that to his parents," Nancy said, annoyed by Trevor's attitude. No wonder Gary had been having problems with him. This guy was a jerk.

"His parents are actually supposed to show up any minute now," Trevor said. "That's going to be a horrible scene. I don't know what to tell them."

Nancy shook her head. "That shouldn't be your job. Wilder has professional counselors who do that." Abruptly, she changed the subject. "I don't want anything, but I would like to look around a little, though. If you don't mind," she added.

Trevor shrugged and busied himself at his desk. "Whatever."

Hesitantly, Nancy began to pick through the papers and envelopes on Gary's desk. She pulled open the desk drawer and saw a letter sitting on the top of a pile of paper. It was from the Aperture Society of America.

"Dear Mr. Friedman, Congratulations! . . ."

She frowned. This was obviously the letter that Gary had received after winning his last photography contest. She wondered if the police had come across this during their investigation.

Then she spotted Mara's name and number scrawled on a piece of scrap paper. A surge of emotion rushed through her. It was so sad that Gary had gotten to take Mara out only one time.

As she sifted through Gary's books, Nancy noticed Trevor watching her. "So, did you talk to the police?" she asked.

"Yup," Trevor said. "They asked me lots of questions about Gary's personal life."

"What did you tell them?" Nancy asked.

"The truth," Trevor replied, a trace of hostility in his voice. "I didn't really know what to tell the cops—he was my friend, but how was I supposed to know what was going through his brain?"

Nancy cocked her head, surprised by Trevor's choice of words. "Your friend? I thought you and Gary didn't say much to each other. Isn't that what you said yesterday?"

"S-Sure," Trevor stammered. "Forget it. I'm sorry. I don't know what I'm saying."

"But you are saying that you actually believe that Gary *did* jump, right? I just want to be clear. Because that's not what I remember you saying yesterday—"

Trevor sat on his desk, swinging his legs. "Did you know he left a note? Did you know that he said his life wasn't worth living? That seems like someone who's determined to do something about his unhappiness, doesn't it?"

"I guess so," Nancy replied hesitantly. But her mind was racing. She remembered what the guy in the hall said. Trevor had come back into the room *after* the police left. After, she assumed, the police took Gary's supposed suicide note with them. So how had he known what the note said?

She phrased her question carefully. "I guess the police let you back in here after they were done."

"And they took forever," Trevor snapped. "I mean, what did they expect to find?"

Nancy got to her feet. Most of her thoughts had been focused on Sean Masters and his threats to Gary. But now, she was getting strange feelings about Trevor, too. "Just one more thing," she said. "You said you were at the chem lab all yesterday morning before Gary was found."

"Yup." Trevor nodded.

"And you didn't come back to the room until after the police left."

"Yup again."

"Thanks," Nancy said as she headed out of the room. "I've got to go. Please give me a call if you want to talk or anything."

Nancy was supposed to meet George at the Cave for a quick lunch. On her way she decided to make a detour to the chem labs, a sprawling bunker of high-tech buildings next to Holliston Stadium. A guard was sitting at a desk by the door.

"You need to sign in, miss," he said, nudging a roll book across the desk.

Nancy turned the page back to Sunday morning and ran her finger down the list of names. Sure enough, Trevor's name was inked in early, long before the time Gary was found. So, it looked as if Trevor had told the truth about where he'd been yesterday morning.

To her surprise, Nancy felt a twinge of disappointment. For a few minutes there, she'd actually thought that Trevor held the key to what had happened to poor Gary.

" 'And I so surely so suspect'—I mean, '*do* suspect.' I'm sorry, I'm sorry again."

Bess's face was flaming. This was the first rehearsal for *Cat on a Hot Tin Roof,* and it was already a disaster.

Bess had messed up this part six or seven times already. And it had been the same story all afternoon. Bess couldn't understand why. She'd been studying her lines and practicing them endlessly, but now it was almost as though she'd never even read the play before.

"Okay, Bess," Professor Glasseburg said, a slight note of irritation in her voice. "I think that's it for today."

Bess stood frozen to her spot on the stage, aware of every eye on her. She was even more embarrassed because the stage lights were shining on her in her costume, the tight white slip.

"It doesn't sound as though you or Maggie can take much more today," Professor Glasseburg continued. "I know you can do better than this, Bess, but there's no use wasting the rest of today's rehearsal. We'll try again tomorrow, people."

Bess hurried offstage. She was so embarrassed, she didn't want to see any of the other cast members. She was sure that everyone was thinking her getting the role of Maggie was a big mistake.

Bess was hoping to get back to the dressing room without speaking to anyone. But unfortunately, someone was determined to speak with her.

Daphne Gillman stood with her long, slim frame leaning against the dressing room doorway. There was a cruel smirk on her face.

"Tough rehearsal," Daphne said. "I hope you weren't distracted by what I said to you the other day. I'm sure no one's paying *that* much attention to the—how shall we say—*fit* of your costume."

Without uttering a word, Bess whirled around and almost ran back across the stage. Daphne Gillman had to be one of the nastiest people she'd ever met. As if Bess didn't feel bad enough about blowing the rehearsal!

"What was that all about?" Brian asked, catching up to her.

Bess filled him in.

"Don't worry about Daphne," he said. "She's a prima donna who refuses to accept that you beat her out fair and square."

Square is exactly right, Bess thought, glancing down at herself in her slip.

"Don't let this rehearsal stay with you, Bess," Brian added. "Everyone is allowed mistakes. It happens all the time. Haven't you watched outtakes at the end of a movie?"

"Sure," Bess said. "Except that a play isn't a movie. You don't get to do it over again until it's right."

"But that's exactly the point," Brian argued. "You do. What do you think rehearsal is all about? You'd better make mistakes in rehearsal because if you don't make them there, it means you're saving them all for the performance."

"Oh, Brian," Bess said. Her shoulders sagged. "I was awful."

"So?" Brian asked. "You'll do better next time."

"But Professor Glasseburg probably thinks she's made a huge mistake," Bess continued. "She's also probably wondering why she didn't give the part to Daphne in the first place. I wish I could apologize or something."

"You really want to do that?" Brian asked.

Bess nodded.

"If it will make you feel better, she's right over there," Brian said, pointing down the hall.

"Thanks, Brian," Bess said as she turned away. Bess caught up to the drama coach in the hallway outside her office. "Professor Glasseburg, I just want to say I'm sorry about today."

Professor Glasseburg nodded but didn't say anything.

"I don't know what went wrong," Bess continued.

"An off day," Professor Glasseburg said lightly. "Bess, you know I believe you can do this part," she went on. "That's why I cast you."

"I know," Bess replied. "And I just want *you* to know that I'm going to spend every free minute I have until the next rehearsal working on that part."

"Well, then, I'm sure you'll be perfect." Professor Glasseburg smiled. Then she nodded and disappeared into her office.

"That's right," Bess murmured as she stood staring after the instructor. "I'm going to be perfect—and look perfect, if it's the last thing I do."

George maneuvered her way through the crowd at the Cave to where Nancy was standing next to a warm radiator.

The Cave was George's favorite place to eat on campus. With its black walls, slate tables, and upside-down soda cans glued to the ceiling, it was a pretty cool place to hang out.

"I'm starving," Nancy said as George approached.

"We're waiting for someone else," George told her. "I asked Mara if she wanted to join us. I thought maybe we could talk to her about Sean."

Nancy nodded happily. "Good idea." She filled George in on getting Sean's address, and the scene with Gary's roommate, Trevor.

"He sounds weird," George said.

"He is," Nancy agreed. "He—" She stopped talking abruptly as Mara twisted through the crowd toward them.

"I got a table over there," Mara said, pointing to a table with a green backpack on it. "Come on!"

They bought sandwiches and sodas at the counter, then went over to Mara's table. George and Nancy tried to make small talk about classes and exams and the football team, but Mara's mind was far away. She gazed blankly at the walls through the whole lunch.

Gently George tried to bring up the topic of Sean. "Mara, Nancy and I wanted to ask you something—"

But Mara shook her head. She had something else on her mind. "You know what's really amazing?" she asked. "How incredibly insensitive people can be. *Everyone* is coming up to me asking me if I know why Gary committed suicide." Her eyes filled with tears. "I have no idea why he'd do it—or even if he did."

Nancy changed her mind about questioning Mara. When Mara got up to get a straw for her juice, Nancy leaned over to George. "Maybe it's not the best idea to bring up Sean right now."

George nodded. "Especially since we're asking if she thinks her ex-boyfriend could have something to do with Gary's death."

Mara returned with her straw but didn't bother drinking her juice. Instead she just sat there staring at her food with no interest.

Nancy frowned. Mara seemed grief-stricken, but Nancy's instincts told her that something else was going on, that Mara was hiding something.

CHAPTER 11

"This sure looks nicer than any of the dorms at Wilder," Nancy commented as she pulled her car into the lot of the off-campus apartment complex where Sean Masters lived.

"I guess the university's star athletes get pretty good treatment," Will said dryly from the backseat.

"I'll say," George agreed.

It was Tuesday afternoon, and George and Will had come with Nancy to find out more about Sean Masters.

Will leaned over the front seat as Nancy slowed down. "Where's Masters's house?" he asked. "They all look alike to me."

"I have to say," George began, squinting up at the numbers on the mailboxes, "that I'm not one hundred percent sure we're doing the right thing, Nancy."

"Yeah, I'd rather just grab the goon and drag him to the police," Will growled.

"First of all," Nancy said, pulling the car over to the curb, "being a goon isn't illegal—as far as I know, anyway. And second, we don't know that Sean had anything to do with Gary's death. That's why we're here, you guys," she reminded her friends. "To get proof one way or another."

"Yeah, well, maybe we don't have any proof yet," George said, "but he certainly made some dangerous-sounding threats."

Before Nancy could reply, she spotted the address. "That's it, two doors up. I don't think we should get any closer. Let's just wait."

"For what?" Will asked.

Nancy looked at her watch. "I want to get a peek inside his place. But we don't know if he's home."

Nancy could feel George staring at her.

"Uh, Nan, being a goon may not be illegal, but breaking and entering is. I mean, your father *is* a lawyer, remember?"

Nancy gave her friend a wry smile. "I didn't say anything about *breaking*." She looked at her watch. "It's almost six. He should be going to eat dinner with the rest of the team any minute now—"

Suddenly Will cleared his throat. "Speaking of goons—"

Up ahead, Sean Masters was closing the

front door of a ground-floor apartment. A minute later he got into a pickup truck parked out front and drove off.

"Did I hear anybody say, 'Good instincts, Nan'?" Nancy asked no one in particular.

Slipping the car into Drive, she coasted up to Sean's apartment and pulled into the driveway.

"Now what?" George asked.

"Now we break all his windows," Will said.

"*Why* was it we brought him along, Nan?" George asked, jerking a thumb at Will.

"I'll show you," Nancy replied. "Come with me."

They all climbed out of Nancy's Mustang and casually walked to the back of Sean's apartment.

"Nancy, I'm not letting you break in," George insisted.

"Don't worry, George," Nancy replied calmly. "Will, give me a boost. I just want to *look* in, and then we'll leave, okay?"

George gave her a reluctant nod. "Okay."

Will planted his feet underneath a window and cupped his hands. Nancy stepped on his hands and pulled herself up.

"See anything yet?" George asked.

Nancy pressed her nose against the cold glass and steadied herself by placing one hand on Will's head. "It's his bedroom, I think.

What a slob," she went on. "He's got a mountain of laundry piled against the wall."

"Great, Nan, let's call the police," George said rolling her eyes. "If it really stinks in there, maybe that's a felony."

"He's got posters all over his walls," Nancy reported. "Football and basketball posters mostly. Wait a second. Oh, wow. I don't believe it."

George peered up at her. "What is it?"

Shielding the light from her eyes, Nancy tilted her face to get a better look. "This is really creepy. That's not all Sean has on his walls."

Scattered among the sports posters were dozens of blown-up snapshots of Mara. Mara in a bathing suit. Mara in hiking boots and shorts. Mara in a long gown at a formal dinner with other football players and their dates. Mixed in with the posed shots were several other photos, which Nancy guessed had been taken without Mara's knowing it. Mara on her way to class, clutching her books. Mara laughing on the steps of the Student Union. Mara talking to people, to guys. To Gary!

A shiver ran up Nancy's spine as her eyes landed on a big picture lying on Sean's bed. It was a blowup of Gary—with his eyes gouged out!

For a moment Nancy was so terrified, she couldn't speak.

"Ouch," Will muttered suddenly. "You're pulling my hair out, Nancy!"

"Sorry," Nancy said urgently. "Let me down."

She leaped to the ground and began sprinting toward the car. "Come on, you guys."

"What is it?" Will asked, close on her heels.

"Nan, did you see any evidence?" George demanded.

Nancy's hands felt icy, and her heart was pounding in her chest. "I saw enough to start asking tough questions."

George slammed her door and swung her seat belt across her lap. "Ask tough questions of whom? Sean?"

"Not yet." As she pulled the car away from the curb, Nancy's knuckles were white on the wheel. "Of Mara."

Bess closed her script, stepped to the middle of the room, and sighed.

Thank goodness Leslie was out with Nathan. Bess had managed to convince Leslie to let Nathan take her to the new diner he'd heard about. Greasy food in a goofy place could be fun, Bess had said, with a huge fake smile. Anything to keep Leslie from staying home and studying, or worse, offering to help Bess rehearse.

At the moment Bess preferred to rehearse alone, without anyone watching her. She'd even refused Brian's offer of help, which had probably hurt his feelings. But Bess was feeling so bad about herself that she didn't want anyone around until she had the part down.

Bess took another breath and tried to get into character. The scene she needed to rehearse was one where Maggie's emotions ranged from anger to sorrow to cynicism. It was a very complex scene, and Bess knew she needed all her concentration.

But within seconds after she started the monologue she made a mistake, and then, in her panic, she forgot almost every line she knew. Her stomach growled, and she felt dizzy enough to fall to the floor by her bed.

If only she could get back the feeling she'd had a few days ago, when she'd found out she'd gotten the lead. What a great day! She'd felt totally on top of the world.

Now Bess wanted to cry. She was so frustrated, she felt like ripping up the script page by page.

Instead she reached angrily under her bed and pulled out her shoe box of snacks. She ripped open a candy bar and began eating furiously.

Her mind was racing. She began reciting Maggie's lines to herself over and over. But by the time she'd calmed down, fifteen minutes later, it was too late. Bess winced. She'd done it again.

All around her on the floor were empty wrappers, cellophane bags, and crumbs from cookies and chips.

"This is disgusting," Bess said, a wave of revulsion washing over her. "I can't believe I just ate all this—junk!"

Bess dropped her head into her hands, her long blond hair falling down on either side of her.

You've got to stop this, she told herself remorsefully.

An image of Daphne flashed in her mind. Daphne smirking as Bess stood onstage, the seams of her slip split open and her thick waist peeking out.

"No way is that going to happen," Bess vowed, lifting herself off the floor and quickly throwing away all the signs of her binge.

"I cannot break my diet again," Bess told herself. "I cannot gain any weight right now."

Bess went to her closet and reached in for the plastic bucket she kept all her toiletries in.

"I'm not going to let the junk I ate ruin me," Bess decided. "There's only one thing to do."

Resolutely, she pulled her toothbrush and toothpaste from the bucket. Then she left her room and went down the hall toward the bathroom.

"There's more to do here at Wilder than in all of Moscow," Nadia said enthusiastically.

Jake beamed down at her. "Everything's an adventure for you, isn't it?"

It was nine o'clock on Tuesday night, and Jake was crossing the campus with his arm draped over Nadia's slim shoulders. They'd just spent another evening together, this time at the Underground, the on-campus alternative music bar, listening to folk music.

Nadia rested her head on Jake's shoulder. "I feel like I'm on an enchanted journey."

"I'm glad. Me, too," he said. "We're so lucky. . . ." His voice trailed off as the memory of what had happened to Gary ambushed him again. He still couldn't believe his friend from the *Times* was gone.

"I know," Nadia said softly. Both of them were still haunted by the memorial service for Gary, which had taken place at the *Wilder Times* office the night before.

The service had been totally heartbreaking. Gail had found some of the best photos Gary had taken for the paper—some serious, some funny—and blown them up as a reminder of how he had found pictures for all their words. Lots of the staff had stood up to talk about how much fun it had been to work with Gary.

"I just can't get Gary out of my mind," Jake went on. "I worked with him at the newspaper since I started there. It'll be so weird not having him around, cracking dumb jokes and trying to hit on freshman girls."

Nadia held his hand, not saying anything until they reached Thayer Hall. Then she turned to face him.

"I don't want this night to end," Jake said, drawing her close.

"Those are my wishes, too," Nadia replied.

She looked up at him, and Jake wondered if he was reading her right. Was she inviting him upstairs? Nervously, he looked through the door toward the elevator that he'd taken to the third floor, to suite 301, a hundred times.

There's nothing to be nervous about, he told himself. Nancy had told Nadia she didn't mind that the two of them were dating. In fact, Nadia had said that Nancy actually seemed glad.

"Where's Casey tonight?" Jake asked.

"She's sleeping at the Kappa house."

"Oh." Jake peered up at the night sky, at the million pinpricks of light. He leaned down and put his mouth close to Nadia's ear. "You want me to come upstairs?"

Nadia nodded. "But if you are too upset, I understand," she said.

"You're sure?" Jake whispered.

Again, a decisive nod.

There was no time for him to make a decision. It felt, to Jake, as if the decision had been made for him. Jake was tugged, firmly but gently, through the lobby and into the elevator. In the car, Nadia pressed a button, and the number three lit up.

It was the same floor, but tonight a new chapter in his life was opening while another finally closed.

CHAPTER 12

From far in the distance, Jake heard several high-pitched bleeps, rhythmic and urgent. They reminded him of a hospital—as if he were tied to a life-support system. As if every breath depended on his waking up.

His eyes flew open. It was his watch alarm, chirping beneath the bedcovers. Sometime in the night he'd remembered to set it for seven A.M. Now he quickly shut it off.

His eyes roamed over the strange room. Pictures of Casey's boyfriend, Charley Stern, hung on the wall. Nadia's clothes were flung over a chair. The strange and beautiful scent of her perfume saturated the air.

He knew exactly where he was, what he'd done, and with whom—and he couldn't be happier.

Turning on his side, he kissed Nadia on the

cheek. Her bed was narrow, but they'd slept through the night in each other's arms.

Watching her sleep, watching her breathe in and out, in and out, he felt as if he'd found an angel. "Do I love you?" he asked her, relieved she couldn't hear him—or answer.

Through the wall, he heard someone else's alarm and felt a surge of anxiety.

Last night he'd managed to push aside his anxiety, but now he was concerned about being here in Nancy's suite—right across the hall from Nancy's room.

I've got to get out of here before I bump into her, he thought. Jake slipped out from under the covers and into his clothes.

Nadia didn't have any notebooks or paper on her desk, so Jake borrowed an index card from Casey's and scrawled a note.

Sorry I had to leave so early. Last night was magic. You're magic. I'll call you later. Yours (I hope), Jake.

He picked up his cowboy boots, watching Nadia the whole way as he backed out through the door. . . .

Nancy lay in bed wide-eyed, her hands behind her head, unable to sleep.

Thoughts churned in her head.

I wish Mara had been in her room last night

when George, Will, and I went over there, she thought for the hundredth time.

Mara had hinted that Sean had sometimes been physical with her, and Nancy really wanted to know if Sean had a history of abusive behavior. The bizarre photo of Gary with his eyes scratched out had haunted Nancy all night. If she couldn't track Mara down and question her this morning, it was time to go to the police.

Nancy glanced at her clock. It was seven A.M. Across the room, Kara was sound asleep. She thought she heard a noise coming from Casey and Nadia's room, which was odd. Nancy knew that Casey had spent the night at the Kappa house, and Nadia had late classes, so she'd still be asleep.

"Well, I may as well catch up on the reading I didn't do this weekend," Nancy said to herself.

She pulled on her terry-cloth robe and stepped into her slippers, then reached under her desk for her bathroom pail. It was stocked with toothbrush and toothpaste, makeup, and shampoo.

She quietly unlocked the door and stepped into the hall. As she turned toward the bathroom, she bumped into something in the middle of the floor. "What—" someone cried, and Nancy gasped.

"Hey!" she said. "Who's— Jake?" she added in surprise.

In the dim light, Nancy saw that the large object was actually a person. Jake was bending over, pulling on his boots.

"I'm really sorry, Nancy," he said, standing up. He raked his fingers through his hair, trying to straighten it.

"Don't bother, Jake," Nancy said, smiling. One of the things she'd always liked about Jake was his permanently casual state. With his cowboy boots and blue jeans, the messy hair was all part of his style. "But what are you doing—?"

As soon as she said the words she knew the answer. Slowly, her eyes left Jake's face and traveled along the wall, stopping on the door to Casey's room. And Nadia's room.

Nancy could feel her face heat up with embarrassment and nervousness.

"I was, uh, hoping I could slip out before you got up," Jake confessed, obviously flustered.

"Thanks for thinking of me," Nancy said sharply. Instantly she regretted her tone. *What's wrong with you?* she chided herself. *He has every right to be here.*

"Look . . ." Jake gestured first at Nadia's room, then at Nancy's. "If this is too weird or awkward, you know, I don't have to come over here. I mean, Nadia and I could—" Then, exasperated, he just stopped and waved his hand, as if erasing his own words. "I'm sure you don't really care what I do anymore, but if it's a problem, let us know."

Nancy shook her head slowly. "I told Nadia it was cool with me. But I guess it's weirder than I thought it would be," she blurted out.

"It's pretty weird for me, too," he admitted.

The two of them stood there staring at each other, not quite knowing what to say. Then Jake cleared his throat and turned around. "I'll see you later," he murmured.

"Okay," Nancy replied. She remained frozen as the suite door closed behind him and the sound of his footsteps echoed down the hall on the way to the elevator.

Why couldn't you have stayed in your room for five more minutes? she thought, slumping against the wall. Then you would have never seen him.

"I'm glad I caught you," George said, handing Nancy a cup of coffee.

George had been waiting outside the entrance to Mara's dorm. It was eight-thirty, and students on their way to their nine o'clock classes were streaming by.

"When I got Mara on the phone, I told her we'd be right over. I didn't want to lose the chance to talk to her," George explained.

"Great," Nancy said unenthusiastically.

George could see something wasn't so great with Nancy.

"Nan, are you okay?" George asked gently. "Is all of this upsetting you?"

Nancy shook her head, then nodded. "No. I mean, yes. Everything's bothering me," she blurted out. "And to top it all off, I ran into Jake this morning."

"Already?" George exclaimed. "I thought he was a dedicated sleep-in kind of guy. Don't tell me he's changed his sleeping habits?"

Nancy smiled wryly. "In a manner of speaking. Not necessarily the time," she said, "but the location."

"I get it!" George said. "You mean, you ran into Jake coming out of—"

"Nadia's room," Nancy finished. "Casey slept at the Kappa house last night."

George gave Nancy's arm a squeeze. "Ouch. That must have hurt."

"It bothered me a lot more than I thought it would," Nancy admitted. "And I feel like I acted like a jerk."

"I doubt that," George said. "But to tell you the truth, Nan," George said softly, "I never understood why you broke up with Jake."

Nancy took a deep breath. "It just wasn't working," she started. "That long weekend, when Jake went home with me, I realized that we were on different wavelengths and— Oh, never mind," she said abruptly. "My relationship with Jake is dead and buried. That's all that really matters."

George eyed her. I'm not so sure, she thought. She'd never been convinced that the reason they broke up was because of something wrong between them. It had always seemed more like Nancy was blaming Jake for her problem with her father and his new girlfriend. George wasn't about to tell Nancy what she thought because she didn't think Nancy was ready to hear it. Besides, she reminded herself, the two of them were trying to get to the bottom of what happened to Gary Friedman. "Come on," George said, putting an arm around her friend. "We'd better go in before Mara changes her mind."

Nancy nodded. "Since you know her a little better," she suggested, "why don't you bring up Sean?"

"Sure," George agreed. She knocked on the door to Mara's room.

When Mara answered, she looked better than she had in days. She was nicely dressed in a long, formfitting black jumper and a long-sleeved white T-shirt. Her hair was pulled back in a ponytail.

"You look great," George remarked. "You must be feeling better."

Mara smiled and let them in. "I've been doing a lot of thinking in the last day or two about Gary. Whatever happened, I had no control over it. I have to stop blaming myself."

George threw Nancy a look of surprise as they all took seats. "Why would you blame yourself? Gary was so psyched you guys were going out."

Immediately Mara became flustered.

"Mara," George said, touching her friend's knee. "We wanted to ask you about Sean."

"What about Sean?" Mara snapped.

"Like, have you ever seen him get angry—" George began.

"Well, he does play defensive line on the football team," Mara pointed out. "He's angry the whole game."

"We mean angry off the field," Nancy put in.

Mara shrugged. "Sure, I guess. Sean was built for physical contact. I mean, just look at him."

"Did he ever hit *you?*" George asked gently. "Or get violent with you?"

Mara bit her lip. She shrugged. "Once or twice, he kind of lost his cool. But why are we talking about Sean? I thought you guys wanted to talk about Gary."

"We *are* talking about Gary," Nancy said. She looked over at George.

"What Nancy's saying"—George took over—"is that Sean threatened Gary. And we want to know if there was any way that Sean could have pushed Gary out that window," she finished.

Mara's mouth dropped open, and her face went beet red. "No way!"

"Mara," Nancy said softly. "George and I think that you've been hiding something. Did Sean say something to you about Gary?"

"If you're trying to protect him, you're not," George chimed in. "As more time goes by the worse it gets. And Nancy and I are going to the police after we finish talking with you."

Mara's eyes went wide, and George watched her swallow hard. "There's something I haven't been telling you guys," she said, facing them both. "I wasn't going to tell you, but now . . ." She took a deep breath as tears sprang into her eyes.

"Sean is a violent guy," she went on. "I've always known that. He knew that Gary and I had gone out on Friday night, and he was really mad. In fact, he was furious. But he couldn't have pushed Gary out that window."

"How do you know for sure?" Nancy asked. "Sean had no problem threatening Gary and Will or pushing George around—"

Mara took a deep breath. "Because he was with me on Sunday morning."

George and Nancy looked at each other in astonishment.

"Sean was with *you?*" Nancy said.

Mara nodded. "Sean and I were together on

Saturday night and Sunday morning, here, in this room. Right here. I was supposed to see Gary on Saturday night, but I canceled on him that night. I told him I wasn't feeling well."

"Why?" George blinked in surprise.

"I wanted a little time," Mara said. "I'd just broken up with Sean, and even though I liked Gary a lot, I wasn't ready to get too intense."

George still couldn't believe what Mara was saying. "But you spent the night with Sean?"

Mara was crying hard now. Nancy offered her a box of tissues, and Mara tore a few off the top.

"Sean kept calling. That night I didn't answer his phone calls so he ran all over campus trying to track me down."

George nodded, remembering the way Sean had demanded to know where Mara was at Club Z.

"When he came back to my room around midnight and started knocking, I let him in," Mara went on.

"I know it sounds stupid, but you have to understand something: There are sides to Sean that you don't see. He can be gentle, kind, even funny. He was begging me to give him another chance, and I spent the whole night talking with him, trying to decide what to do."

Nancy was pacing the room. George could tell by her expression that she was trying to sort everything out.

"So what did you decide?" George asked Mara.

Mara straightened up in her chair. "I told Sean that it was over. I wanted to give my relationship with Gary a chance. And you know what?" she asked. "Sean didn't yell, he didn't scream, he didn't even put up a fight. It was the saddest I've ever seen him, but he just left."

"So Sean was nowhere near Gary's dorm that morning?" Nancy said. Mara shook her head. "Then Sean had nothing to do with Gary's death," she went on.

"But this doesn't mean Gary killed himself, does it?" Mara asked.

George was unsure, but Nancy wasn't. "Gary did *not* kill himself. I thought Sean might have had something to do with it, but even if he didn't, there has to be another answer. And I've got to find out what it is."

Later that afternoon Nancy was back in suite 301, getting her research organized for a paper on William Faulkner.

She was happy that everyone in the suite was either in the library or in class. As much as Nancy loved all of her roommates, there were times when she needed silence and calm.

Nancy was trying to concentrate on her paper, but what she'd found out that day nagged at her.

Nancy had been sure that Sean Masters was responsible for Gary's death. He'd had the motive and certainly the temper.

But now that Mara had admitted to being with him and had provided an alibi for him— Sean was cleared. Gary's roommate, Trevor, had been somewhere else, too. So who . . . ?

Just then Nancy heard a door close in the hallway. Someone in her suite was still around. Moments later Nancy heard a voice in the lounge. But there was only one voice. Whoever it was must be on the phone, Nancy thought.

She didn't mean to eavesdrop, but the suite and the dorm were so quiet, she couldn't help it. The voice coming from the other room was speaking in a foreign language.

It's Nadia, Nancy realized. She was mesmerized by the sounds of the unfamiliar Russian language. In Nadia's deep, rich voice, it sounded very exotic and, Nancy had to admit, very sexy. No wonder Jake's attracted to her, Nancy thought.

Finally it sounded as if Nadia was getting off the phone. There was silence for a minute, and then a loud kissing noise. And then suddenly, Nancy heard Nadia say in English, "I love you, too."

Nancy smiled. Nadia must be talking to her parents. She wondered what they thought of their daughter being so far away in America.

But after a few more kissing noises and another softly murmured "I love you," Nancy changed her mind. There was no way Nadia was speaking to her parents.

But hadn't Nadia told everyone in the suite that she didn't have a boyfriend back home?

And what about Jake? Nancy wondered. As far as she knew, Jake didn't know a word of Russian.

Nancy's heart stopped for a second. She'd been jealous of Jake and Nadia this morning, but now she only felt worry and concern—for Jake. She cared a lot about him and didn't want to see him hurt.

The door to the suite closed, and Nancy heard Nadia walk down the hall.

I've got two mysteries to solve, she decided. First, she had to find out what had really happened to Gary.

And then she was going to find out the identity of Nadia's mystery man.

CHAPTER 13

The next morning Nancy slouched in a chair in the far corner of the lecture hall during her journalism class. Professor McCall had spent an hour lecturing about the power of the press in presidential campaigns, how reporters can shape their readers' thoughts about the candidates. It was an important and interesting idea, one that usually fascinated Nancy. But instead of listening and asking lots of questions, Nancy was busy jotting notes to herself about Gary and Trevor.

I don't even know why I bothered to show up for class, she thought.

Finally Professor McCall dismissed class, and Nancy bent down to pick up her backpack. As she shoved her notebook into the bag, the bag slipped off the desk and landed on the floor with a thud.

Nancy sighed. "It's going to be that kind of

day," she mumbled, watching the contents spill all over the floor. Pens and pencils and pennies were rolling down the aisle.

Nancy bent down to gather up her things. As she began stuffing things back into her backpack, she noticed something at her feet. Her heart skipped a beat.

"I forgot all about this," she murmured. She picked up the small black canister and looked at it. It was Gary's canister of film, and his shattered camera was still at the bottom of her backpack. "I can't believe I never gave this to the police."

Still holding the small canister, Nancy grabbed her backpack and scrambled up the steps and out the door. She quickly navigated through the crowd in the hall, desperate to get to the campus security office. But halfway across the quad, she stopped dead in her tracks.

She opened her hand and stared at the little black canister again. Convinced that it might hold some of the answers to her questions, Nancy whirled around and hurried off toward the *Wilder Times* office.

Her walk became a jog, then a run, then a flat-out sprint.

The darkroom at the *Wilder Times* office was an oasis from the buzz of activity in the newsroom. Jake was happy to get away for a few minutes. Outside, all anyone could talk about was Gary's death. Besides that, Gail had assigned several stories on suicide, so that Wilder students could learn more about the presence of counselors on campus and the suicide hotlines for people who were feeling depressed. Jake was glad that the paper was doing something about the problem, but Gary's death was still hard to deal with, especially since he had been a friend.

Jake was cleaning up some supplies when Nancy stepped into the room. "Oh," he mumbled. "Hi." It was the first time he'd seen her since bumping into her the morning before.

"Hello," Nancy said, equally surprised.

She brushed past him and started lining up the bottles of chemicals she'd need to develop film.

"What's the rush?" he asked.

Nancy didn't reply.

"Do you need some help, Nance?" he asked. "I've never seen you develop film before."

Nancy was carefully reading a poster with printed instructions. "I've done it before," she said. "I'm sure I can do it again."

Jake couldn't let it go. He was too curious to know what she was up to. "What's on the film?" he asked. "Something for your Women in Athletics story?"

Nancy suddenly looked up. Jake couldn't read the expression on her face, but it almost seemed as if she was deciding whether or not to trust him.

Jake couldn't help feeling a little hurt. "We used to do this stuff together," he said quietly.

Nancy's whole expression softened. "You're right," she said. "I'm sorry, Jake," she added. "I'm just kind of tense. And running into you yesterday morning wasn't exactly the world's most comfortable experience."

Jake could only nod.

"The reason I'm here," Nancy said, placing a small black canister on the counter, "is to develop this film. It's the last roll of pictures that Gary shot."

"What?" Jake stared at her as she worked. "Where did you find it?" In the red lights it was hard to tell, but Jake thought Nancy was blushing. "Nancy," he went on, "are you sure you're the one who's supposed to be developing this film?"

"Uh"—Nancy hesitated—"in a way, I do think I'm the one who should be developing it."

Jake could see her swallowing hard as she shook the can containing the film and the chemicals.

"The day Gary died, his camera was lying there in the grass near him," she went on. "The police overlooked it. I was going to give it to them. I just—"

"Forgot," Jake finished the line. "How convenient."

"I really did forget," Nancy said, folding her arms across her chest. "And when I remembered . . . Well, tell me you wouldn't have done the same thing," she challenged him.

"No comment," Jake said, flashing her a lazy grin.

"We have to keep this between us," Nancy said. "You know what I mean, Jake. Until we see what's in these pictures and what they mean."

"Don't get your hopes up," he warned her. "They might not hold any answers."

Nancy looked at him, and suddenly it was all Jake could do not to step across the few feet of space that separated them and take her in his arms—just as he had done so many times before. But their relationship was over, and Jake was crazy about Nadia, and yet, there was still this pull toward Nancy.

Chill out, Collins, he told himself. Reluctantly, he looked away and waited for the negatives to develop and dry.

Then he watched as Nancy went to work making prints from the negatives. They both stood staring into the tray, waiting for images to appear on the paper Nancy had placed in it.

"Come on," Nancy murmured. "Show us a clue, any clue."

Jake laughed. "You haven't changed one bit," he said affectionately.

Nancy raised her eyes to his. "You have."

Jake lifted his eyebrows, then lowered them. He nodded reluctantly. "I have a bit," he admitted. "Does it feel weird, standing here like this with me?"

"Not really." Nancy shrugged. "Does it for you?"

Jake shook his head. "It feels nice. I like you, Nancy. I'm not angry or anything."

"Good." She smiled at him. "Then we can be friends."

Jake was about to say something back, but something made him stop. For the first time since they broke up, they were standing in companionable silence, and it felt really good. Jake hadn't realized until this moment how upset he'd been about losing Nancy's friendship on top of everything else. Maybe they could start again—as friends.

"So, as a friend, can I tell you something?" she asked.

Jake nodded. "Shoot."

"I like Nadia a lot, I really do," she said softly.

"But?" Jake looked at her quizzically.

"But maybe you should take your time," she

blurted out. "Don't get involved so quickly. You don't know her that well, after all."

Jake blinked, trying to understand where she was coming from. Nancy had just said they could be friends. So, why was she giving him a hard time about Nadia now? Was she jealous or wasn't she?

"Thanks for the advice," Jake finally replied. "But you don't have to worry about me. I know what I'm doing."

Nancy's lips trembled, as if she had something else to say. Then Jake could see her abruptly change her mind as she turned toward the trays instead.

"Look," she said. "The pictures are ready."

Jake helped her fish out the photos and carefully pin them to the clothesline stretched over their heads. Together they stood back and studied them.

Jake first saw a few photos of a very attractive dark-haired girl in a tennis outfit.

"Who's that?" he asked.

"Mara Lindon." Nancy sighed. "Someone he had a crush on since he saw her at freshman orientation. She's organizing the History of Women's Athletics exhibit."

"Oh," Jake replied. "So she was the girl he'd just started dating."

"Right." Nancy pointed to a few of the other photos. "This was a rugby game we went to on Saturday."

"What are these?" Jake asked, moving toward the next batch of pictures. "They look like they were taken inside a dorm room."

Nancy focused on the shots of a room with a bed and a dresser. She recognized several of Gary's things strewn about the room. "He was working on a photo essay on campus housing," she remembered. "Maybe he was using his own room as a subject."

"How thrilling." Jake rolled his eyes, then looked at the last picture. "Now, this one's weird. It's all blurry, as if the camera wasn't focused."

Nancy glanced at the photo, bringing it closer to her face. "What is it?"

"Well," Jake said, "it looks like a blurred close-up of someone wearing a baseball cap. There are the eyes, and there's the bill of the cap. It's a Toledo Mudhens cap." Jake shrugged. "Looks like a mistake to me."

But obviously, Nancy didn't think so. "That's no mistake," she murmured as she stared at the shot. "It's a clue. An important clue!" Jake felt her grip his arm. "I think I know what happened to Gary!"

As Nancy held the photo in both hands, her body was seized with anxiety and fear.

"What do you mean, 'it's a clue'?" Jake asked.

"That baseball cap is Trevor's," she said. "He's Gary's roommate."

"So?" Jake shrugged. "Gary was probably taking pictures of his room. Maybe he took this one just to be goofy."

Nancy shook her head from side to side. "No, listen to me, Jake," she said, going back to the rugby photos. "Here, look, this is Saturday during the day, right?"

Jake nodded.

"Then here's the next one, of Gary's room. It looks like night, right? All the lights are on, and the windows are dark."

"Okay—" Jake said.

"Then these next ones of the room were taken in *daylight,* so this one must be Sunday morning."

Jake was nodding. "I'm with you. But I don't see the significance—"

Nancy was motioning with her hands as she spoke. "The last picture he took was of Trevor with his baseball cap, right? But it's Sunday morning, which means that Trevor had to be there."

"Obviously," Jake stated.

Nancy stared at him. "But Trevor told me he was at the chem lab all morning. He said that he left before Gary woke up and didn't return until the police were gone."

Jake looked puzzled. "But if Gary took his picture, Trevor had to have been there."

"Exactly!" Nancy said. "Now, you tell me: Why would Trevor have lied?"

Jake turned to meet her gaze. "He must have something to hide."

Nancy nodded. "And I think . . ." She snatched the photograph and tore it off the line.

"Where are you going?" Jake called after her.

"Come on, we have to ask a guard an important question," she said, and burst out of the darkroom.

Nancy led Jake out of the office and across the quad toward the chemistry labs. "What does a guard know?" Jake asked, struggling to keep up with her.

"Hopefully nothing," Nancy said out of breath.

Jake shook his head. "I don't get it."

Nancy pushed through the entrance of the lab. "Watch and listen," she said.

Luckily, the same guard she'd seen on duty on Sunday was seated behind the desk. He was wearing a campus police uniform with a badge and a hat. "Good morning," he said. "Please sign in."

"Actually," Nancy said, "we have something to ask you instead. I saw you on duty Sunday. Do you know Trevor McClain?"

The guard broke into a broad smile. "Trev?

Of course. He practically lives here. We eat lunch together sometimes. He's a very studious young man. In all my years at Wilder, I've met very few students who care about their studies as much as Trevor does."

"And you saw him Sunday morning?" Nancy asked the man.

The guard nodded. "Yes, I did. Very early. In fact, weren't you the young lady I showed the sign-in book to?"

Nancy nodded. "And he was signed in," she said.

"But here's the question," Jake broke in, obviously following Nancy's train of thought. "Do you know when he left?"

"That's an easy one," the guard said. "When everyone else did. We had a minor accident here that morning. Someone didn't screw the cap on a bottle of chemicals tightly enough, and some of it spilled. Sometime after Trevor arrived, I think, the fumes got so bad we had to clear the building. Everyone was gone. We had to get some technicians in here to clean up."

Nancy's eyes widened. "And there's no way Trevor could have stayed?"

The guard shook his head. "We're very strict about regulations, especially with so much toxic material around. I saw Trev leave myself." He raised his hand, pointing. "In fact, we were standing right out there on the grass.

163

About seven-thirty, I guess it was, the technicians came out and told us it would take at least an hour or two to clean up. Trev said he was going back to his room."

Nancy grabbed Jake's hand and gave it a hard squeeze. "Thank you," she said to the guard.

Outside in the sunshine, all Jake could say was "Wow."

"Double wow," Nancy added. "Trevor must have been the one who—"

"Not necessarily, Nancy," Jake broke in. "We know Trevor was in the room that morning, and that he lied. But we weren't in that room when Gary fell. We don't know what happened."

"But I think I have a pretty good idea," Nancy replied, and headed toward the administration building.

"Where are we going?" Jake asked.

"To see the dean," Nancy declared.

As she walked, she told Jake everything Gary had told her about Trevor's obsession with grades, and about how Trevor was in a total zone when it came to his work. Nothing else existed. Nothing else was important.

"Gary was thinking about switching rooms, it was so bad," she added.

"Of course!" Jake broke in. "Let's not forget the university's roommate suicide policy. If a student dies or commits suicide, his or her roommate gets an automatic four-point-oh grade point average for the semester."

Nancy gave Jake a punch in the arm. "Don't you ever read articles in the *Times* besides your own? That rumor was exposed as totally false weeks ago. There's no such policy at Wilder. But wait a minute. Are you telling me that you think Trevor McClain murdered Gary for a four-point-oh GPA?"

"Maybe," Jake said. "Maybe he didn't read the *Times* article."

"Well," Nancy said with an air of finality, "we're about to find out."

An hour later Nancy and Jake were sitting in the waiting room outside the dean's office. They'd explained everything they knew and everything they believed to be true. They had shown the dean the photo of the guy in the Mudhens cap and had told him what the guard at the chemistry lab had said.

After that the dean had picked up the phone and told Nancy and Jake to wait outside his office.

Nancy felt her stomach clench as the waiting-room door opened and Trevor McClain stepped inside. "Hey!" He did a double take when he saw Nancy. "What are you doing here?"

Nancy lowered her eyes. She couldn't look

at him. If, in fact, he had killed Gary, he'd murdered one of her good friends.

Jake rested a consoling hand on her shoulder.

The dean opened his door and signaled the three students to enter. Trevor silently walked past Jake and Nancy.

"He looks terrible," Jake whispered to Nancy as they followed Trevor inside. "He looks like he hasn't slept in days."

"Good," she shot back under her breath. "Neither have I." She closed the door behind them.

The dean stood behind his desk. He was a tall man with wire-rimmed glasses. "Maybe we'd better all sit down," he said, motioning them to the chairs opposite his desk. After everyone took a seat, he pushed the blurry close-up of the man in the baseball cap across the desk. "Mr. McClain, do you recognize this photo?"

"No. What are you talking about?"

The dean cleared his throat. "Isn't that your room and your baseball cap?"

Trevor seemed about to deny it, but when he opened his mouth, no sound came out.

"I know you weren't at the lab Sunday morning for more than a few minutes, Trevor," Nancy said, jumping in. "Gary took that picture just before you pushed him, didn't he?"

Trevor covered his face in his hands and

began to sob. "It was an accident. I didn't mean it."

The dean picked up the phone and asked for campus security. He said a few words, then replaced the receiver.

"What happened, Trevor?" the dean asked.

Nancy saw that Trevor's hands were trembling violently as he tried to compose himself. "Gary was sitting on the window ledge, and I was standing over there," he said, lifting his arm and pointing, as if he were back in his dorm room. "Gary was trying to get a wide-angle shot of the room. He was telling me what a slacker I was, how I didn't work hard enough, how he was worried that I was going to flunk out of school. I mean, he was joking with me. I think he was trying to lighten things up. I'm so tense all the time. He was just playing around."

"So, did you push him?" the dean asked.

Trevor shook his head. "It wasn't like that. What happened was—" Trevor rose from his chair and walked trancelike to the window. "I was laughing, and he was making these goofy jokes and playing around. I'm not sure when he took that picture, but we started wrestling, you know, like kids . . ."

Trevor froze. "Then he just fell," he whispered. "He lost his balance. The expression on his face—it was as if he couldn't believe it."

Nancy glanced at Jake, who was riveted on Trevor.

"I didn't mean it, Dean. It wasn't what you think."

Nancy felt tears streaming down her face. What had those final moments been like for Gary? He must have been terrified. But if Trevor hadn't planned the whole thing, then . . . "What about the suicide note?" she asked.

Trevor lowered himself onto a couch. "It was stupid. I wanted to call for help, but I was an idiot. I was scared. My parents put so much pressure on me. Straight A's, perfect test scores. They won't accept anything less. You see, I remembered the four-point-oh policy for students whose roommates commit suicide—"

"So you typed a suicide note?" Jake asked, his voice filled with disgust.

Trevor nodded. "And then I ran down the back stairs to get out of the building until an ambulance came."

Suddenly two campus police appeared in the doorway. The dean rose to his feet. "Young man, I will call your parents. You may not have killed Gary Friedman, but you've obstructed justice at the very least. You have a lot to learn, Mr. McClain, first of which is not to listen to rumors. Wilder has no such grade policy in the case of suicide. Your foolishness makes Mr. Friedman's death an even greater tragedy for the school. Let's hope that Gary's poor parents will find solace in the fact that their son didn't take his own life."

Nancy stared at Trevor's frightened, pale face. "It doesn't seem right that someone who was planning to become a doctor could be so callous about another person's life," she said quietly. "How could you cover up what happened like that?"

"And let everyone think it was a suicide," Jake chimed in.

Trevor just cringed and dropped his head.

Nancy closed her eyes. She could feel Jake's hand in hers, and she could hear his voice, far away, trying to console her. But all she felt now was pain and loneliness.

I'll miss Gary forever, she told herself. But at least we know the truth now.

CHAPTER 14

"You've been staring at that book for over an hour," Kara said to Nancy from across the room. "But you haven't turned a single page. You haven't taken any notes either, for that matter."

"That's because I haven't read a word," Nancy admitted. Finally she snapped the book shut. "I don't know who I'm kidding. I can't concentrate."

"Well, it *is* Friday afternoon," Kara said happily, throwing herself on her bed. "The weekend starts officially in"—she checked her alarm clock—"ten minutes."

"Whoopee," Nancy said sarcastically. She drew a circle in the air with her finger.

Kara ignored her. She jumped up and peered into Nancy's closet. "Let's see, what can I borrow tonight? I'm so bored with my own clothes."

For the first time Nancy smiled. "Kara, I don't think there's a piece of my clothing you *haven't* worn."

Kara pulled out a green sweater. "Do you mind if I borrow this?"

"Nope." Nancy shook her head.

As Kara tried on the sweater, she turned to face Nancy. "So what's up with you, Nance? Are you still bummed out about Gary?"

Nancy nodded. "I really miss him. And that's not going away for a long time." She shook her head. "But to tell you the truth, I'm actually thinking about my dad tonight. It's his birthday, and this is the first time ever that I'm not celebrating with him. Though he's probably having an awesome time with his new girlfriend at some romantic weekend hideaway, sitting by a fire."

"Nance, he has a right to his own life," Kara reminded her.

Nancy wanted to scream. If one more person told her that . . .

Kara seemed to sense it was time to change the subject. "I have to say that I'm not so sure about this Nadia and Jake thing. It's all kind of sudden and intense, don't you think?"

"Yes." Nancy agreed. "But it's not because I'm jealous, it's . . ." She paused, wondering if she should tell Kara what she'd heard in the lounge.

Only if she wanted it broadcast all over campus in the next thirty minutes, she reminded herself. Besides, Nancy realized, she shouldn't jump to any conclusions. "I just want Jake to be careful," she finished.

Suddenly there was a loud knock at the door.

"Will you get it, Kara?" Nancy asked. "I don't feel like seeing anybody."

"Even if he's six four with blond hair and big blue eyes?" Kara asked, eyeing her.

Nancy cocked her head. "Okay, if he's six four," she replied, "but not if he's shorter."

As Kara swung the door open, Nancy heard a muffled laugh.

"Well, he's not six four," Kara reported. "I'd say he's closer to six feet even."

"What?" Nancy went over to look at who was standing in her doorway.

"Surprise!" loud voices shouted out at once. Nancy gasped. Dozens of people wearing party hats stood in the hallway outside Nancy and Kara's door.

"Oh my gosh," she mumbled as she realized they were all the people she'd invited to her father's party—the party she'd canceled. And standing in front with an arm around Avery was her father himself. As Nancy stepped toward him, she burst into tears.

"It was all Avery's idea," Carson Drew said, taking his daughter into his arms.

Nancy looked at Avery. Her soft brown hair fell in loose curls around her shoulders, and her green eyes twinkled. She gave Nancy a big smile.

Shame washed over Nancy. No wonder Dad is crazy about Avery, she mused. What a thoughtful thing for her to do.

Nancy reached out to give Avery a hug. "Thank you," she said.

Avery hugged her back. "You're welcome."

Then Nancy grabbed her father's hand. "Come on, Dad. Let's party!"

It was definitely weird for Bess to see a bunch of adults hanging out in the hallway of suite 301. But from the expressions on their faces, Bess could tell they were having fun. They were probably reminiscing about their own college years.

"Isn't this strange?" George whispered, echoing her cousin's thoughts. "I never thought I'd be hanging out with Nancy's dad in a college suite."

"I know, I know." Bess laughed. "But I'm so happy for Nancy that this happened."

"Me, too," George agreed. "And at least at this party, we're not limited to dining-hall food! Come on, let's go chow down."

Bess didn't reply as she followed George over to the card tables, which Avery and Hannah had set up to hold all the food.

"Aren't you going to have anything, Bess?" George asked, heaping a paper plate with a sandwich, pasta salad, and several homemade brownies.

"I don't think so," Bess mumbled, trying to ignore the hunger pangs in her stomach. She'd been so good all day; she just couldn't lose control now.

"Why not?" George asked, juggling her plate as two of Mr. Drew's lawyer friends brushed past her.

"I have something else to do," Bess said.

"On a Friday night?" George sounded suspicious. "What's up?"

"N-nothing," Bess stammered. "Really. It's just . . . Before Avery called to tell me about the party, I'd promised Brian I'd go over lines with him." Bess was afraid her cousin would see through her lie. "We have our next big rehearsal soon, and he's really nervous about his part."

"Oh," George said. "That's too bad."

Bess nodded. "Will you tell Nancy I had to go?"

"Sure," George replied.

Bess gave her cousin a quick hug before she began making her way to the door. Just keep smiling, Bess, she told herself. Until you get out of here, just keep smiling.

As she stepped out into the night air, Bess

was thinking about finding an empty practice room in Hewlitt and working on her monologues. She wanted to be perfect during the next rehearsal.

But then she remembered that her script, with all her notes in it, was sitting on her bed.

Even though Bess tried not to think about it, she couldn't help but picture what else was waiting for her in her room. Just below her bed.

A shoe box full of goodies.

Nancy rested against the wall of the lounge, marveling at the sight—just about every important person in her life was jammed into her suite, laughing, dancing, having a blast. It was a dream come true.

"Your dad's awesome," Dawn said, passing by with a platter of cheese puffs.

"And hot!" Casey whispered. "Too bad I'm already engaged."

"Too bad my dad's already taken!" Nancy shot back, laughing.

She caught her father's eye across the room and gave him a wave. He winked back and blew a kiss.

"I've never seen him happier," someone said.

Avery stood beside her now, beautiful in a black dress and balancing a plate of brownies and minimuffins. "Want one?" she asked, grinning. "I baked them myself."

"In that case—sure," Nancy said, and tossed a minimuffin into her mouth. "Wow," she said, "they are good!"

Avery smiled. "Maybe not as good as Hannah's—but close," she replied.

"No one can beat Hannah's cooking," Nancy said.

"That's for sure," Avery put in, smiling. "I've given up trying to compete with her."

Nancy's eyes traveled back to her dad, who was dancing with Kara. "My dad looks great. Has he lost some weight?" she commented.

Avery's eyes shone. "I make him jog with me every morning," she said. "But you know, I don't think I've ever seen him happier," she went on. "And that's because he's here with you, Nancy."

Nancy blinked, surprised by her warm words. Slowly she turned to the other woman. "I haven't exactly been the most understanding human being on the planet, have I?"

"Nooo," Avery began with a wry smile. "On the other hand, I'm not sure how understanding I'd be, either. You've had a lot to deal with in the last few months: leaving home, breaking up with your first serious boyfriend, and getting used to a new life. I'm sure it would have been nice to know that everything you left behind at home was going to stay just as you left it."

Nancy stared at her. "That's *exactly* what I've been feeling!" she said. "How did you know?"

Avery laughed. "A lucky guess," she said, shrugging.

Nancy looked at Avery thoughtfully. "I guess the selfish part of me wanted to stay the most important person in my dad's life."

"But you are, Nancy," Avery assured her. "Your father and I love each other, but you are his one and only daughter. And . . ." Avery swallowed, her eyes moistening. "I'll never be able to—or want to—take the place of your mother. Never, ever."

Nancy nodded, her own eyes filling with tears.

"I'm sure she was a wonderful woman," Avery said softly. "I just want to be your friend."

Nancy brushed away her tears. "I know that now," she murmured. "And I'm sorry I've been so difficult. Dad and I have always been very close, and I couldn't help thinking that I had lost that. I—I understand now that you weren't trying to push me out. And I think we could be good friends."

"Me, too," Avery agreed, smiling warmly.

Just then Nancy noticed her father watching them cautiously.

"Dad has no idea what we've been talking about," she said to Avery.

"Judging by the look on his face," Avery said with a laugh, "he thinks we're arguing again!" Suddenly Nancy put her arm through Avery's, and together both women waved at Carson. Relief passed over his face.

"I think that this is the best birthday present we could have given your father," Avery said.

"I couldn't agree more," Nancy said. She blew her father a kiss, then mouthed the words "Happy birthday, Dad. I love you!"

Nadia sat on the couch in the suite's lounge watching all of the activity around her.

People wearing hats and waving streamers bobbed around her. Snacks went by on big platters and music was blasting from Casey's stereo. Right now Nancy Drew was dancing to a CD by a band called Nirvana—with her father!

It was a sight that made Nadia want to laugh—and cry. She'd never danced with her father like that. She would never have even thought of it. But here—it all seemed so easy and carefree.

Nadia cocked her head. It was still amazing

to her that she was sitting on this couch, in these clothes, in this country. Home was very, very far away.

Thinking of home reminded her of something else. Nervously, she checked her watch.

She was expecting a call from Russia. How could she possibly talk with all this racket? Nadia wondered. A flare of anger went through her. Her phone calls from him were all she had, the only way she could stay in touch with him, for who knew how long? She hadn't expected anyone to be hanging around the suite on a Friday night. She'd have to get her own phone in her room.

Suddenly the phone did ring. Nadia almost couldn't hear it through the din around her. She jumped up, but Dawn Steiger was already answering it. A minute later Dawn turned to her.

"Nadia?" Dawn shouted out. "I *think* it's for you, but I'm not sure."

"Thanks," Nadia replied.

"Hello," she cried into the phone. "It's me, darling," she went on in Russian. "I love you so, and I miss you. But I can't talk right now—"

"Nadia?" a male voice interrupted her. She instantly recognized it. It was Jake. "Nadia? It's me, Jake. That is you, isn't it? I'm going to learn Russian, I promise." He laughed. "I just haven't picked it up yet."

"Oh, Jake!" Nadia said, shaking her head. Her heart pounded as she realized she had just made a nearly fatal mistake. "How glad I am that you called," she continued. "I was just thinking of you."

"And I haven't stopped thinking of you," Jake replied. "What's going on over there? Are you having a party without me?"

"No, no," Nadia said quickly. "This is a party of Nancy's. Her father is here."

"Oh." Jake sounded surprised. "Then I guess it's not a great idea for me to come over then."

"Maybe not," Nadia agreed. "But that doesn't mean I can't leave. I would love to see you, Jake."

"Really?"

Nadia could hear the happiness in his voice, and she smiled.

"You're sure you weren't expecting another call?" Jake asked. "A call from home?"

"Of course not," Nadia assured him. She forced a laugh. "I just feel so close to you already, I forgot you couldn't speak my language."

Jake chuckled softly. "There's another language we speak together," he replied. "Pretty well, I think."

"I think so, too," Nadia agreed.

"Why don't you meet me downstairs in five

minutes," Jake said. "We'll do something fun."

"Sure—okay," she said. Slowly Nadia hung up the phone. She stared at it for a few seconds. Then she sighed and turned toward her room for her coat.

NEXT IN NANCY DREW ON CAMPUS™:

TV station WWST is devoting an hour to campus news and views, and Nancy's running the show—maybe. First, she has to deal with Michael Giannelli. He's smart, he's handsome, and he's got an ego the size of Lake Michigan. And he thinks *he's* running the show. But that's just one of the items setting Wilder U. abuzz. . . . Item: Who has a shocking announcement to make about the new girl in his life? Item: Who's looking to add excitement to her marriage, even if it means going to extremes? Item: And whose life could secretly spin out of control unless Nancy intervenes? Stay tuned: Big stories are coming to a boil, and the truth is about to come out . . . in *Otherwise Engaged,* Nancy Drew on Campus #23.

Nancy Drew on Campus™

By Carolyn Keene

- ☐ 1 New Lives, New Loves — 52737-1/$3.99
- ☐ 2 On Her Own — 52741-X/$3.99
- ☐ 3 Don't Look Back — 52744-4/$3.99
- ☐ 4 Tell Me The Truth — 52745-2/$3.99
- ☐ 5 Secret Rules — 52746-0/$3.99
- ☐ 6 It's Your Move — 52748-7/$3.99
- ☐ 7 False Friends — 52751-7/$3.99
- ☐ 8 Getting Closer — 52754-1/$3.99
- ☐ 9 Broken Promises — 52757-6/$3.99
- ☐ 10 Party Weekend — 52758-4/$3.99
- ☐ 11 In the Name of Love — 52759-2/$3.99
- ☐ 12 Just the Two of Us — 52764-9/$3.99
- ☐ 13 Campus Exposures — 56802-7/$3.99
- ☐ 14 Hard to Get — 56803-5/$3.99
- ☐ 15 Loving and Losing — 56804-3/$3.99
- ☐ 16 Going Home — 56805-1/$3.99
- ☐ 17 New Beginnings — 56806-X/$3.99
- ☐ 18 Keeping Secrets — 56807-8/$3.99
- ☐ 19 Love On-Line — 00211-2/$3.99
- ☐ 20 Jealous Feelings — 00212-0/$3.99
- ☐ 21 Love and Betrayal — 00213-9/$3.99
- ☐ 22 In and Out of Love — 00214-7/$3.99

 Available from Archway Paperbacks

Boys. Clothes. Popularity. Whatever!

**Based on the major motion picture from Paramount
A novel by H.B. Gilmour
53631-1/$4.99**

Cher Negotiates New York 56868-X/$4.99
An American Betty in Paris 56869-8/$4.99
Achieving Personal Perfection 56870-1/$4.99
Cher's Guide to...Whatever 56865-5/$4.99

And Based on the ABC-TV Prime Time Series

Cher Goes Enviro-Mental 00324-0/$3.99
Baldwin From Another Planet 00325-9/$3.99
Too Hottie To Handle 01160-X/$3.99
Cher and Cher Alike 01161-8/$3.99

Simon & Schuster Mail Order
200 Old Tappan Rd., Old Tappan, N.J. 07675
Please send me the books I have checked above. I am enclosing $_____ (please add $0.75 to cover the postage and handling for each order. Please add appropriate sales tax). Send check or money order--no cash or C.O.D.'s please. Allow up to six weeks for delivery. For purchase over $10.00 you may use VISA: card number, expiration date and customer signature must be included.

POCKET
BOOKS

Name _____

Address _____

City _____ State/Zip _____

VISA Card # _____ Exp.Date _____

Signature _____ 1202-05